TEN SLEEP

C.W. SMITH

In Memory of Griff, Ross, Travis, Kyler and Dutch

In the years I've spent studying ethnobotany, one plant species in particular has inspired me on a personal level as much as a scientific one: the poppy. Its unlikely emergence from the ground and subsequent flowering has come to symbolize to me that in despair there can be hope, that being buried can herald a beautiful bloom if dug up and given a little sun.

—Skinny Pete, introduction of unpublished PhD thesis

Chapter One

Lyle Rogers coaxed his Ford up the steep switchbacks that cut through Ten Sleep Canyon. He pressed the accelerator further to the floor as the grade increased but the old Ford groaned at his request, burdened by the horse trailer in tow. The switchbacks in front were barely visible in the dim moonlight, but Lyle knew the turns well from countless trips up and down this mountain pass. As he approached the first hairpin, he rolled down the window and lit a smoke. He had a long night ahead of him, determined to make Denver by dawn. He sank further into the Ford's tattered seat and tried to find a better signal on the AM radio. The reception was always better at night for reasons he didn't really remember, something to do with reflections or the atmosphere or maybe even government regulations—it didn't really matter. He tuned to a station playing Jimmie Roger's "Gambling Bar Room Blues" and turned up the volume, static and all. He sighed as Jimmie and the rumbling Windsor V8 slackened his thoughts. He took a few more drags from his cigarette before pitching the still-burning butt out the window.

The canyon above him was lined with cliffs of dolomitic limestone hundreds of feet high; a small creek meandered through the canyon bottom far below. It was hard to imagine the creek was responsible for the creation of this dramatic landscape, but it was also hard to imagine the authority that a million years can carry. While the last century was insignificant to the rock, river, and pinion, much about the area had changed. Gone were the Crow, Sioux, and Shoshone tribes. Gone were the buffalo and grizzly bear. New were highways, black Angus, and jack pumps.

To the natives a century ago, the region was the midway point between the Great Sioux camp on the Platte River to the south and another camp to the north near the Clarks Fork River. The area marked a ten-day voyage, or *ten sleeps*, to each. Unlike most geographical designations bestowed by native tribes, the name was retained by their invaders. Now, distances were measured in miles rather than sunsets and locals ride in pickup trucks instead of on horses, but Ten Sleep was still a place that people mostly just passed through.

A recent onslaught of rock climbers and whitewater kayakers to the area had meant a change of pace to the formerly sleepy, and still quite drowsy, town and highway. A quiet truce had been found between the liberal, hedonist recreational tourists and the conservative local ranchers and farmers, partially due to the money the tourists brought to the local economy and the occasional anxiety the locals' sidearms brought the tourists. Lyle thought most of the recent changes were for the worse.

Headlights in the rearview mirror interrupted his meditation. The vehicle behind was approaching quickly, it's lights bigger and brighter every time he looked back. He slowed down and nudged his pickup and trailer to the shoulder of the road to allow the vehicle to pass—anyone driving that fast at this time of night couldn't be trusted.

As the truck behind overtook Lyle's from the left lane, it swerved hard to the right and hit the Ford behind the driver side door. Lyle reacted impulsively, almost jackknifing the trailer with his response. The truck came at him again and hit hard, pushing Lyle further onto the narrow shoulder. He was being squeezed between the ramming truck and the edge of the road, itself bordered by an escarpment dropping down to the river a half-mile below. Lyle pressed his foot further into the pedal in an attempt to pull away, but his pickup could go no faster. Its tires kicked up gravel as they slipped near the edge. Lyle struggled to pull the pickup back onto the pavement.

The truck behind surged at him again, knocking Lyle into the driver's side door with its impact. He fought back, trying to match the charging truck with a blow of his own, but the trailer was too cumbersome and heavy to maneuver quickly. The two vehicles were rapidly approaching the next switchback—if he couldn't make the turn, the fall off its edge would surely kill him. He stomped on the pickup's spongy brake pedal as the truck swerved at him once more.

Gunshots echoed off the canyon walls.

Chapter Two

S kinny! Come hit this spliff before it's cashed!"
Jeb leaned back in his camp chair next to the fire ring, pinching the remnants of a joint between his fingers. "Seriously Pete, it's almost gone." Jeb rested the joint between his lips while he tucked a wiry black dreadlock into his stocking cap and closed the top buttons on his flannel shirt. The setting sun cast long shadows through their cluttered campsite, the fire beginning to illuminate the branches of the conifer trees surrounding them.

Pete sat in the open door of a dented orange van applying salve to his tender fingertips, sore from the days spent climbing the canyon's sharp limestone. Pete's curly blond hair billowed out of the bottom of his trucker hat, whose peeling patch stated *I Pee In Pools*. When he was younger, Pete's friends began calling him Skinny Pete due to his tall, sinewy frame, perfect for rock climbing. After almost a year of living in the van together, Jeb was beginning to think that Stinky Pete might be a more appropriate nickname.

"Still can't believe that *whipper* you took today, man," said Jeb, "biggest fall I've seen for a while. Maybe a twenty-footer, huh?"

Pete walked over to the cooler, his stride lanky, and grabbed another can of beer. "Yeah, I thought I had it in the bag so I skipped that last clip. Guess I'll have to go back tomorrow and try to climb it clean. Think I got it next go." Pete opened the lukewarm beer and took a gulp. The informal ethics of climbing demanded that a route be climbed without falling for it to count, although nobody agrees on exactly what it counts for. While neither Pete nor Jeb had anything to gain or lose with their ascents or failures, Pete felt a particularly strong need to adhere to this decades-old matter of ideology. It was only a small part of the paradoxes in principle that he seemed to live by.

"Let's get on *Roughneck Rugburn* tomorrow. That route looks rad. Maybe we could wander over there after you send your project," said Jeb as Pete retook his seat next to him and the fire. "Throw another log on there, Skinny. It's getting cold."

Pete grabbed the remains of the joint from Jeb and took a short pull before throwing it in the fire. He picked up another section of split wood and leaned it against the others in the pit. As the effects of the joint settled in, Pete unconsciously pulled on his patchy blond beard and let his mind wander. The two sat quietly for a moment, entranced by the flickering flames. They had been climbing together for many years and sharing the van as their mobile home for almost one, so both had become comfortable with long periods of silence.

Jeb finally spoke, "Ghosts, man. Ever think about that? We're the ghosts of society. Nobody sees us, nobody even knows we're here. We just quietly roam around, in our own world. Once in a while, sure, our world overlaps with the real one, but then— boom! We are gone again." Jeb clapped his hands together to emphasize his point. "Two dudes living in a van, climbing everyday—no money, no real jobs, no real footprint." Jeb paused, appreciating the cleverness of his own simile. He laughed, the weed obviously working. "We're like Casper the fucking ghost, man. Casper Jeb and Spooky Pete, climber ghosts of the West."

Pete giggled softly, "Spooky Pete—that's way better than Skinny or Stinky." Pete looked at Jeb as his grin grew wider. "I am going to be light as a fucking ghost when I float up *Grandpa Has a Tramp Stamp* tomorrow!" Pete's giggle erupted into full laughter, soon joined by Jeb. "That route is going down!"

"*Go* Spooky, *go!*" Jeb pantomimed frantic climbing movement, his hands scratching above his head for the next imaginary hold.

"*Venga* Casper, *venga!*" Pete yelled in a strained Spanish accent. Their laughter grew uncontrollable as Jeb's pantomime became even more frenetic.

"*Allez* Spooky, *allez!*" Jeb shouted in French inflection. The pair's laughter became uncontrollable. Pete tried to take a sip of beer when he caught his breath, only to choke on it as he began to giggle again.

His laughter cut off as the sounds of gunshots and

deforming metal rattled through their campsite. The pair looked at each other, startled.

"What the fuck was that?" Jeb suddenly felt sober, momentarily frozen by the surreality of the sounds.

"I don't know. Get your headlamp." Pete stood from his chair and picked up the hatchet that was propped against the wood pile.

The two set off into the dark toward the highway, a lone beam of light illuminating the sagebrush in front of them. Part of being a climber is the foolhardy notion that danger is relative. Another commonly held notion—but equally false—is that if you can climb, you can do anything.

***

"It's no use, Pete. He's dead." Jeb sat on a rock above the wreckage, rubbing his eyes and shaking his head in disbelief. Pete frantically pushed his palms into the man's chest, who seemed to have been thrown clear of the truck sometime in its roll down to the creek. "It's not his breathing that's the problem—look at all of the fucking blood."

"Fuck fuck fuck!" Pete yelled, finally stopping his chest compressions. "What do we do?"

The pair had been trying to resuscitate the man since arriving on the scene. His shirt was saturated in blood, which now covered Pete's hands as well. Neither had seen a dead body before, much less tried to revive one. The dark canyon suddenly seemed a very different place than it had that morning, before the coffee, climbing, joints, beer, and laughter. Time was different, too. Was it slower, or was it just more *slippery*? Pete didn't know if he had been hovering over the body for one minute or twenty.

"I guess we better call the cops. Maybe drive down canyon until our phones work, call it in from there," Jeb said, shaking his head in disbelief. "This is fucked."

Pete tried to wipe some of the blood off his hands on the thick prairie grass. He grunted as he stood up and walked over to Jeb. "I didn't sign up for this shit. Is it even safe for us to call the cops? What if they want to talk to us, like at the station, or search the van?"

"Relax. It's just a car wreck, and we just happened to be camped across the creek from it. That guy was probably drunk anyway. Let's drive down the canyon, call it in, then get some beers at the Two Bit. Erase this night from our heads." Jeb stood up and put his arm around Pete, patting him on the back.

"Thanks. You're right. I've just never..." Pete's voice faltered as his headlamp's beam flashed across the horse trailer, laying on its side just uphill from them. It had broken free from the truck in the roll down the hillside. "Fuck." He looked at Jeb ominously. "Do you think the horse is still in there?"

Jeb looked back up the hill at the horse trailer. "I can't deal with anything else dead right now." He shivered as he contemplated what might be waiting for them inside. "Let's leave it for the cops. We better go call this in." He patted Pete on the shoulder as they walked back down the hill and across the creek to their campsite.

Chapter Three

The Two Bit Saloon housed a menagerie of dead and dusty animals on its walls, trophies of a modern pastime that was an occupation a century earlier. A dozen mule deer mounts hung above the bar, proudly shot by the former bar owner but now known as *The Disciples* by a few irreverent local patrons. The walls were sheeted with old barnwood, and the bartop itself was cut from the center of a single cottonwood tree. For visitors it would be easy to assume that the construction and decor of the saloon was intended to look Western and charming—in fact, it was built with what happened to be available.

Deputy Burl Hutchinson sat at the bar, a half-eaten plate of fries in front of him, wearing a dark wool vest over a faded flannel shirt. He was approaching the age where most people retire, but his limited finances didn't leave that as an option. His grey stubble hid most of the lines of his years, although he wasn't as fit as he thought he should be, a growing belly and weakening legs his biggest complaint.

Burl was technically off duty, but in a one-deputy county he never kept strict hours. Even so, he refrained from having the *one last* beer he desperately wanted. The saloon's patrons were mostly roughnecks, ranchers, and truckers, but the town had its share of Evangelicals and Mormons as well, neither of whom would appreciate rumors of their deputy being publicly intoxicated—especially considering his past struggles with sobriety.

While he finished his dinner, his attention skipped between the PRCA bull riding event on the TV and the bartender Sunny overtly flirting with a man at the bar that Burl recognized but didn't know well. The man had moved to town last summer, and Burl had a habit of greeting transplants with suspicion. He hoped the man respected Sunny and Lyle's marriage, as rocky as it had become, but he had his doubts. The man's polished handsomeness heightened Burl's misgivings. He tried to listen in on their conversation, but the rowdy hollers of the roughnecks playing pool behind him made eavesdropping difficult.

"Burl," Sunny called out from down the bar, flipping her highlighted blonde hair over her shoulder, "another round for you?" She snubbed out her lipstick-smudged cigarette in an ashtray and walked closer to Burl. Her heavy makeup obscured a naturally beautiful face, even if it was starting to show the inevitable signs of age. Burl had always been attracted to Sunny, but given his friendship with Lyle, he kept his feelings buried as deeply as he could.

"No thanks, I best be getting on my way. Long morning at the courthouse tomorrow. That Manderson boy is going on trial you know. Worst part of my job." Burl nudged the plate closer to the far edge of the bar. "Tell Jim the burger was mighty fine, as always. Put it on my tab, if you would."

"It's on the house tonight," said Sunny.

"You shouldn't. But I appreciate it." Burl finished the remaining sip of beer from his glass. "You seem pretty interested in talking with Slick down there. Love that fringed jacket he's wearing." Burl looked down the bar at the man with disdain, rolling his eyes.

"Who, Monty?" Sunny laughed, wiping down the bar top in front of Burl. "You should get to know him. Been all over the world, tons of interesting stories. Even lived in the Bahamas for a spell. You aren't jealous of my attention, are ya?" Sunny met eyes with Burl, her lips pursed sideways.

Burl blushed and looked away. "Where's your rotten husband tonight? I expected to see him down here."

"Lyle is on his way to Denver tonight. Dropping off a horse for Sergeant Cole at the auction tomorrow. Cole has him running all over the country these days for those damn horses." Sunny squeezed out the bar towel into the sink. "Says he's making good money, at least. Promised to take me to the Keys when he saves up enough. God, to see the ocean."

"Fair enough. The Keys sound nice, wouldn't mind getting out of here for a bit myself." Burl scratched his head as he tried to remember the last time he had taken a vacation or left Wyoming.

"Haven't seen the ocean since my honeymoon. Forty something years ago, I guess." Burl pushed the memory from his head before he became emotional. "Never been to Florida, though."

Sunny looked warmly at Burl, noticing his watering eyes. "You know they eat sea snails in the Keys? Conch, I think it's called. Supposed to be pretty good, battered and fried. Washed down with a margarita, of course."

Burl shook his head. "Count me out. If you want to eat snails, I've got plenty in the garden."

Sunny laughed. "Very sophisticated, Burl. Don't you want to get out and see the world? I can't wait to get out of this hell hole town- been here too long. Same damn bar, same tired faces." Sunny pulled a cigarette from a pack below the bar and lit it. "Not yours, of course," she said, winking at Burl.

"I'm afraid the more I see of the world, the more I like this little *hell hole,* as you call it." Burl stood up and zipped his jacket, stretching the fabric slightly over his bulging belly. "Goodnight, Sunny. Thanks again for the burger."

"G'night, Burl. Take care."

The deputy nodded as he grabbed his earflap hat off the hook by the entrance. He pushed back his tousled gray hair and seated the hat on his head before walking out the door. As he neared his truck, he felt the buzzing of his pager—a familiar sensation, but never a welcome one. *Dispatch,* Burl thought, *looks like my night ain't over.* He unlocked the truck door and got inside, grabbing the radio off the dash.

"Hello, Marlene, Burl here. Just got your page."

The raspy voice of the dispatcher cut through the static of the radio. "Hey Burl, sorry to bother you with this, I know you are off duty, but Sheriff Dawes is out on a domestic call and we got a report of a car wreck on Highway 16, up canyon. I radioed the Worland medics, but I figured you were probably in Ten Sleep already and might get up there faster."

"Roger that. I'll head up there now."

Burl grumbled as he started his truck and headed toward the canyon. It was the last thing he wanted to be doing.

Chapter Four

Jeb hung up his phone when the 911 operator asked for his name, thinking that Pete's instinct to stay anonymous had merit. The pair sat in silence in the van, pulled off the road just below the mouth of the canyon where cell phone service had first returned. Jeb looked over at Pete and shrugged. "Beers?"

Pete shook his head to signal otherwise. "I can't stop thinking about that trailer—what if there was a horse in there, and it's still alive? The dead guy is beyond our help, but we might be able to help the horse."

Jeb laughed. "Who are you, Doctor Fucking Doolittle? I don't know shit about horses and I suspect you don't either."

Pete cocked his head to acknowledge Jeb's point. "True. Let's go take a look anyway. It's just up the road. The beers will taste better knowing we tried."

Jeb sighed. "Ok, you win. Let's go rescue a fucking horse." He turned the van around and the pair headed back up Highway 16.

***

Pete and Jeb parked the van back at their campsite before crossing the creek and heading back up the hill to the crash site. Jeb ran up the steep slope below the horse trailer, hoping to prove that their mission was futile. The trailer was on its side, the downhill edge resting precariously on the limestone boulder that had stopped its roll. The rear doors had torn open and hay bales protruded out the back. Jeb grabbed a door to help pull himself close enough to look in, causing the trailer to rock toward him.

"Whoa, sketchy!" He stepped further around the downhill door, out of its way if the trailer were to tip further. He pointed his headlamp into the back opening. "No horse in here," he yelled to Pete, "just some hay and a couple of boxes. Careful, it feels like it wants to roll." He sat down on the hay bale to catch his breath, tired from his sprint up the hill.

Pete caught up and sat next to Jeb. "Guess we caught a little bit of luck at least," he said, breathing heavily.

The pair rested silently, trying to process the events of the evening. Jeb took a joint from his shirt pocket, searching his jeans for a lighter. He lit the joint and after a long pull from it, he slid one of the battered boxes over to his perch on the bale.

A soft breeze blew down through the canyon, rustling the leaves on the cottonwoods. The moon was about to break over the rim of the canyon, its light making the low clouds glow. Time began to feel right again. Jeb opened the box.

"Dude," Jeb smiled as he passed the box over to Pete. "I think we caught a bit more than luck." Pete peered in, staring wide-eyed at the hundreds of small packets of white powder.

"Fuck. That's drugs, right?" Pete glared at Jeb incredulously.

"No bro—that's a million bucks," Jeb said, his eyes gleaming.

Headlights from an approaching vehicle flashed around the corner of the switchback below. "Time to go," Jeb said, stacking one box on top of the other and tucking them under his arm.

"What are you doing? We aren't taking those."

"Sure we are. We'll talk about it back at camp." Jeb started scrambling down the hill toward their campsite before turning his head back toward Pete. "Turn off your headlamp. We're ghosts, right? We were never here."

***

As the moon reached its apex for the evening, Pete and Jeb slept tenuously in the van, each fidgeting in their respective narrow beds. Pete's restlessness was due to worry, while Jeb's was from the excitement of the plans he couldn't help but make. The pair's unrest was mirrored outside as the nocturnal animals in the forest around them began to forage. From above it might appear that they were staging a coordinated offensive—a coyote, a fox, and a multitude of squirrels, all scurrying—but in fact they were merely searching for their nightly meal. It was normal night in Ten Sleep Canyon, but a normal night that few people ever see. Common events never witnessed seem anomalous and strange, but mistaking the mundane for the remarkable is what makes magic. Morning found the animals home in their dens and Jeb and Pete back in their camp chairs, basking in the morning sun.

"Are you sure it's heroin?" Pete asked Jeb as he examined the contents of the boxes. "I always thought heroin was a bit yellow. Guess I don't know, never seen it before."

Jeb was shirtless, the day already warm enough to go without. His dark complexion hid the depth of his tan, and while he was more muscular than Pete, his torso was still very lean. "Pretty sure. My old climbing partner up in Squamish used to dabble in it before he cleaned up. I think the pure stuff is white. You remember Dan, right? Climbed with him at Index a few years ago. All of Dan's junk looked just like this." Jeb took a sip of coffee and sighed. "Never tried it, never will, but I saw a lot of it sitting around his place. Besides, I think cocaine makes your mouth numb." Jeb stuck his tongue out as he pressed a finger onto it. *"Thith tuff duthant. Thnot at tall."*

"Stop it," Pete said, "We are into some serious shit here. We shouldn't have taken it, it's too much heat. I think we should toss it."

Jeb looked up, his face suddenly serious. "We're sitting on our dreams here, Skinny. If we sell this stuff we will have cash for years. Don't know about you, but I'm almost out of money. Another month and I'll need to find some work." Jeb grabbed one of the baggies, bouncing it in his hand. "Gotta be a few pounds altogether, right? Worth some coin. No more washing dishes, digging in dumpsters. Nothing but climbing for us, my man." Jeb's smile was back. "Yosemite, J-Tree, Red Rocks, the New, the Red, the Gunks, the Bugs, Alaska. Man, we could even go to Tonsai, or Arapiles, even Ceuse. We could get one of those Euro camper vans and drive it back home. Road trip of the century! This is it, Pete—everything we've ever wanted."

Pete shook his head. "What about the...morality...of it? People could die from this stuff. How do we justify that?"

"Suppose we did flush it, bury it, whatever—do you really think it would change anything? Dealers and users will find it somewhere else. The supply is endless as long as there is a demand. You remember the War on Drugs—it hurt the innocent and only made the cartels richer. If you want to save the lives of addicts, there are more effective ways than throwing away our future."

Pete exhaled a slow sigh. "Maybe. But how are we going to sell it? I don't know anyone that uses junk. Way outside my circles. Getting busted with a nickel-bag of weed is a long way from a few pounds of heroin." Pete paused and looked away, his face pale. "I don't even like saying the word."

"I had an idea last night," Jeb said. "We call up Dan in Vancouver, I bet he still has connections. We offload it to him, let him figure out how to sell it and give him a cut of the cash for his efforts. Besides, I'm sick of the heat here and it's prime time for climbing in Squamish." Jeb grinned and looked at Pete. "I bet you wouldn't mind seeing Lydia again, am I right?"

Pete smiled for the first time that morning. Maybe even blushed. "Squamish does sound pretty nice." Pete thought about the last time he had seen Lydia, in Joshua Tree. She had declined his invitation to keep traveling with him and Jeb, instead deciding to go back to the comfort of her home and business of running a coffee shop in Squamish. Pete suspected that she wanted more comfort and security than his current lifestyle could offer. Maybe a windfall could show her that he was more than a poor dirtbag living in a van? He was almost out of money and dreaded the idea of washing dishes again.

Pete's eyes brightened as he rationalized the plan. "You're talking about Dan Jeffries—the *Danimal*? He seems pretty stand-up. I trust you on this one. It would be good to see Lydia. We haven't talked much recently. I hope she still wants to see me."

"Great—Squamish it is," Jeb said. "But let's stick around here long enough to give *B is for Buggery* a few more tries."

"For sure," Pete said, knocking his knuckles into Jeb's, trying to hide his apprehension.

Chapter Five

It had been five days since Lyle's death and Burl had only started to grieve. His first reaction was sympathy for Sunny, followed by personal sorrow over the loss of a friend. Sheriff Dawes, as callous as he sometimes was, assigned Burl to the accident investigation, temporarily muddling his emotions with professional duty. Now Burl was struggling to untangle his sadness from the sudden reminder of his own mortality. He walked into his office and shut the door behind him before noticing the light on his ancient answering machine was blinking red. The machine crackled as Burl pressed the play button.

"Hey Burl, Paul Rigby, Washakie county coroner's office. We found something interesting with Lyle—didn't see it for a while, due to the number of open wounds and all, but right in the middle of one of them I found a bullet. It didn't kill him—looks like that was the head trauma." Paul exhaled a raspy wheeze that was audible in the recording. "I'll send the bullet up to the crime lab in Cheyenne, at least they might tell you the caliber. Good luck, Burl—I think you got an investigation on your hands." The answering machine beeped at the end of the message.

Burl sat down at his desk chair, his legs weakened by the news. "Lord Almighty," he uttered, staring blankly across his office. *Lyle had been murdered.* What had been sad and tragic but understandable was now senseless, and Burl was overcome by sadness that he thought he was no longer capable of.

He'd lost friends in Vietnam, he'd lost his parents to age, he'd lost his wife to cancer. He thought that he had finished grieving these deaths many years ago, but Lyle's murder had brought them back to the surface, a deep splinter finding its way back to the skin.

***

Burl knocked on a white farmhouse door outside Worland, hoping Cole was home. The house sat near a stand of cottonwood trees in an otherwise treeless desert. It had been built by Cole's grandfather, James Herman, in the early 1900's, after irrigation channels connected the area to water but before the railroad connected Worland to civilization. The soil in the Bighorn Basin was alkaline and sandy, but James was able to grow enough alfalfa for a small herd of sheep. He managed to narrowly avoid bankruptcy through the years but couldn't avoid age, eventually passing down the sheep ranch to his son, Roy. Roy was an enterprising man, and frustrated with the calamitous economics of sheep ranching, hatched an idea to profit from the natural hot springs common in the basin. He built a greenhouse plumbed with hot water radiators, keeping the inside temperature suitable for growing tomatoes year-round. The idea was a success and eventually Cole took over the business, expanding the operation to over an acre of geothermally-heated greenhouse space.

"Morning Deputy," Cole Herman said as he opened the door. He was a physically intimidating man, between his size, demeanor, and tapestry of tattoos covering his arms. Despite being retired from the military, his dark black hair was still trimmed in the typical high-and-tight style. "Come on in."

"Morning Sergeant," Burl said, "Thanks for meeting with me. Real sorry about Lyle, I know he'd been working for you for a while. He was a good man."

"Yes, he was," he said, crossing his arms. "Just *Cole*, Deputy. I'm not a sergeant anymore." His face showed little emotion.

"You can take the man out of the military, but you can't take the military out of the man, right? 101st airborne for me. 'Nam. Still got my brass hanging in the woodshop." Burl smiled.

Cole's expression was flat. "I remember your war stories, Burl. Don't tell many myself, nothing good came out of my time. That desert changes a guy—I suppose the jungle does too—but I wouldn't go back to that sand pit if my life depended on it. Wyoming sand is hot enough."

Burl smiled uncomfortably. He had always acted proud of his military service, but he knew much of it was a facade given how quickly he had volunteered to fly cargo to avoid any more combat.

"Sounds like the memorial will be next Friday."

Cole nodded solemnly. "Heard that. Not sure I can make it."

Burl fidgeted, placing his hands in his pockets. "How's business? Tomatoes still paying the bills, or are you getting rich on those horses these days?"

"The cutting horses are just a hobby—seems like they cost me more than I make. Afraid I'm not getting rich on the tomatoes, either." Cole retrieved a can of snus from his back pocket, placing a pinch of it in his lip. "Don't mean to rush you, but what brings you by today?"

"Yes—sorry to ramble. I want to talk to you about Lyle. Nothing certain yet, but it looks like it wasn't an accident. You probably knew him as well as anyone outside of Sunny. Can you think of anyone that would have wanted to kill him?"

"I heard he ran off the road. Why would you think someone killed him?"

"Afraid I can't talk much about it until we know more. Lyle was shot by a small caliber before he ran off the road. Sunny said that Lyle was hauling a horse for you that night. Where was he headed?"

"Good Lord. Are you sure?" Cole seemed shaken by the news. He looked at Burl for affirmation. Burl nodded.

"He was taking a mare down to auction in Denver," Cole said. "I've been having him sell horses on top of taking care of the ranch. He was pretty tired of mending fence, and excited to take on some more work with the extra pay and all." Cole put his hands in his pockets. "He did have that run-in with Carlos a few months ago, as I'm sure you know. And then those rumors about Sunny and Monty, but you'd think that Lyle would be the one doing the killing if they were true."

"Yeah, I've heard some mumblings. Can't believe most of what gets said in this town though, right?" Burl looked up at Cole. "Well, that's all I wanted to ask you. Thanks for your time." The two shook hands and Cole turned and opened the door. "Oh yeah," Burl said, "that horse Lyle was hauling—still haven't found her. Wreck must have spooked her pretty good. Hope she wasn't one of them spendy ones of yours. Let me know if she wanders back to the barn." Burl raised his hand and waved goodbye. "Take care, Cole."

CHAPTER SIX

Dan Jeffries was running through an alley in downtown
Vancouver wondering if he was as prepared to die as he had
once believed. The Triads pursuing him seemed intent on killing
him, replacing his conceptual feelings on death with a rather
concrete one: He was scared.

Dan shot a glance behind him and saw no one, but knew it
was foolish to think that he was out of danger. He turned a corner
out of the alley and onto a busy downtown street, slowing to a
walk to attempt to blend in. He'd had deals go bad in the past,
but never like this—guns had been drawn and fired. Dan tried to
slow his breathing, stop the shaking, but his mind was too rattled
to focus. He didn't know why the Triads had turned on him so
suddenly, what he had done to provoke their violence. He
walked briskly through the crowd and ducked into a coffee shop
on a corner at the first opportunity, sitting down at a booth with
a clear view of the front door. He pulled the hood of his sweatshirt
back over his head as his breathing finally slowed. While Dan
didn't know the events that led him to this moment, he suspected
he knew their origin. He flashed back to the beginning—
Thailand.

"Ooohh, Danny. It's your turn, honeeeey," Doa shouted over the
top of the club's unrelenting sound system as she reached out her
pool cue to Dan. She was beautiful, in a Bangkok prostitute sort
of way, but her Thai/Valley Girl compound accent was starting
to irritate him. Her tight black dress and tall leather boots
increased Dan's tolerance for her speech, however, if only

slightly. "This crazy bitch can't sink nothing tonight!" Dao said to her bleached-blond poolmate Hom, who had a similar accent and an even tighter dress.

"OK mate, let's even it up," said Mick, a large-framed Australian that had invited Dan to play as his partner. Dan grabbed the cue from Dao and lined up a shot, which ultimately rattled out of its intended pocket. The six bottles of Singha he had ingested previously were starting to negatively impact his game. He pulled on his long dark beard while he contemplated what had gone wrong with his shot.

"So, you're headed to Tonsai tomorrow, eh?" Mick asked Dan. Mick's Aussie accent softened his imposing appearance. He wasn't as large nor as fit as Dan, but his face told of a life hard lived. "Tonsai isn't real Thailand, ya know, it's a fairytale for tourists and climbers. You should really see more of the country—there's shit here that'll blow your mind."

Dan nodded and handed the cue to Hom. She grabbed it with one hand, and rubbed Dan's muscular shoulder with the other, pressing her body against his. He tried his best to ignore the advance. "Yeah, I wish I had more time," he said to Mick. "I gotta get back to work soon, running low on cash." Dan had been on an expedition to the Karakoram range in Pakistan when bad weather forced him and his partner to reconsider their plans. "I was supposed to be in Pakistan until next week, but my money supply has been running out more quickly than I'd planned. I'm barely going to scratch it back to Canada as is."

"Ohhh, nice shot you little bitch!" said Dao to Hom, who'd just sunk a difficult combo.

"You play pool like you suck dick, you cheap whore!" Hom shouted back to Doa as she sighted in another shot. Mick laughed at the banter—the trio had been acquaintances for a long time. Bangkok is a huge city with a large underworld, but the regular nightclub cast ran in surprisingly small circles. Mick had been a dealer in Bangkok since leaving Australia to avoid a warrant a few years ago, and the clubs of Bangkok were his usual points of operation. Cocaine, Ecstasy, and heroin were Mick's bread and butter, but he could source almost anything if given enough notice. The clubs were where Dao and Hom practiced their trade as well, although neither acknowledged their occupations specifically.

"Mate, I hesitate to ask you this…," Mick said as he lit up a cigarette. "I just met you, after all. But since you said you could use some *bahts*…" Dan turned to face Mick, the topic of money getting his attention. "I've got a package that needs to get delivered in Ao Nang. You 'll pass through there on your way to Tonsai, last bus stop before the boat ride. It's worth twenty-five thousand baht if you're interested." Mick took a deep drag from his smoke, perhaps unconsciously hinting at the seriousness of the mission.

Dan considered the offer. It had been a night of propositions. First, from Mick, for drugs. Then Dao, and later Hom, for their respective services. He had declined them all, politely, so far. Dan knew what the package likely contained, as well as the likely punishment for getting caught, but some cash could mean a full month of climbing on the sunny, sandy beaches of Tonsai. He blinked. It might have been the exact moment that led him to his present situation in Vancouver. But he might have ended up there regardless, as disposition and fate might be one and the same.

***

The streets of Ao Nang were calm compared to Bangkok, but Dan was uneasy. He felt like everyone on the sidewalk was staring at him and perhaps they were. He was pale, slightly sweaty, and walking erratically. He was to meet Kiet at the Muay Thai Stadium for the kickboxing fights and the exchange. *It will be over soon*, he thought. He just needed to flag down a tuk-tuk and get off the streets, then he would feel much more in control. Touts yelling at him, hawking tickets to cobra fights, maitre d's winking at him and imploring him to come into their bar, tailors inviting him to get measured for a new suit—it was chaotic and surreal and certainly wasn't helping his anxiety. A tuk-tuk finally heeded his hail and pulled over. Dan showed the driver a flyer for the fights he had picked up off the street, and the two sped off. Tuk-tuks and motorcycles in Asia follow different traffic rules than their four-wheeled counterparts—not that the four-wheelers follow any recognizable rules themselves. The driver was splitting lanes, running stop lights, and rounding blind corners with only a honk of the horn. *Surely this is more dangerous than delivering drugs*, thought Dan. The tuk-tuk eventually pulled over at the entrance to the stadium—really just a gymnasium—and Dan handed the driver 30 baht. He went inside and headed for seat 28D, as per Mick's instruction.

His contact Kiet was already seated, smoking a hand-rolled cigarette and wearing a Metallica t-shirt. He was much younger than Dan had expected—certainly too young to be legally smoking, even in Thailand, much less dealing drugs. Dan took his seat next to Kiet and gave him a slow nod, not sure what proper drug-exchanging protocol was.

"Dan, man!" said Kiet. "What's up?" Kiet held out his knuckles for a fist bump. Dan awkwardly matched it with a handshake attempt. Dan was expecting a silent, anonymous drop-off, like in movies where suitcases are switched on a park bench. Kiet grabbed the backpack from between Dan's legs and opened it. He took out the mailing envelope and unsealed it.

"Cool, man. Looks good," he said, sliding it into his own backpack. "Mick said he paid you already, but here is a little gift from me." Kiet again offered his fist out to Dan, this time clutching a small clear plastic bag. Dan looked around nervously before taking the baggie from Kiet and placing it in his front shirt pocket.

"Thanks," Dan said, grabbing his backpack and standing up.

"You aren't going to stick around and watch the fights? The third one should be good, Deng is a real killer."

"No, gotta get going, boat to catch. Headed to Tonsai. Thanks though." Dan walked out of the stadium more anxious than when he had entered. He felt like he had a hot ember in his shirt pocket, threatening to burn through.

***

The overhanging tufas and stalactites of Tonsai didn't match Dan's slow, methodical, and graceful style of climbing, but he enjoyed it regardless. The steep routes required powerful movements from hold to hold, and due to the strength required, speed was a higher priority than precision. Falling off the overhanging rock was safe and even fun, and the position over the clear blue water was magical.

Dan fell into an informal, international crew of climbers who seemed to congregate at the beach bar after their respective days out. Days turned into weeks, and Dan was as vibrant and as happy as he had ever been. The burning ember, however, was still in his possession. From time to time, he took it out from his duffle and looked at it, curious of its use and how it might feel. Fear had prevented him from trying it initially, but late one night curiosity overcame his trepidation. With shaky hands, he rolled up a 50-baht banknote and laid out a small, tidy line of powder.

The effects settled in slowly, more of a sunset than the supernova he expected. Dan melted into his bed, his mind spinning into a swirling, dark tunnel. The burn he felt from his raw fingertips disappeared, as did the pain in his elbows caused by his overused tendons. His thoughts disappeared. He hung in stasis near the edge of unconsciousness before eventually succumbing to sleep.

In the morning, he felt deep guilt and embarrassment. He hadn't enjoyed the experience like he had with some of his other experimentations, and he knew the recklessness of heroin over past drugs. He sipped his coffee in the sun, convinced that it had been a dream; that it had never happened. Somehow, he wanted to do it again.

Dan stood up from his seat in the Vancouver coffee shop, his legs stiff from his frantic run. He wiped one lingering bead of sweat from his forehead and pushed his pockets back deeper into his jeans. He opened the shop's front door, pausing for a moment to scan the street before stepping out into the smog and sounds of the Vancouver afternoon.

CHAPTER SEVEN

Pete hadn't slept well the night before so he made Jeb drive the first leg of their long trip to Squamish. He was lying in the back bed of the van, still too worried about their plan and their package to nap. Pete sat upright, perusing the van's makeshift bookshelf for something to read. Sandwiched between Jeb's precious *Korean Cuisine Made Simple* and Vonnegut's *The Sirens of Titan* was a copy of his own doctoral thesis, complete but never submitted.

Pete had been a semester or two away from graduating when he decided to quit. His research was complete and his thesis written, all that remained were the inevitable revisions and a successful defense. But he couldn't escape the feeling that he had already extracted everything he needed from the experience, and that another degree or certificate only meant being one step closer to life as some machine's internal cog. He bailed, as he had many times before while climbing ambitious objectives, and for similar reasons—it simply was no longer worth it. He walked away from his research and his writing, hoping to travel the world, experience foreign places and cultures, and climb as much as he could. Growing up in a conservative small town under loving but reserved parents, and spending all his adult life so far in school, the thought of living wild and free seduced him.

It didn't happen as he hoped it might, money being the first obstacle. Traveling was expensive, and meager wages meant too much time spent working. The solution was to live on less, even if it meant compromising his exotic dreams. Pete also realized that between being an inexperienced traveler and occasionally prone to loneliness, he didn't want to travel alone. He met Jeb in Yosemite, washing dishes at the lodge. Jeb invited him to the southwest deserts at the end of the tourist season and Pete agreed, finding comfort in Jeb's blithe acceptance of life's challenges. While southern Utah wasn't the international adventure Pete dreamt of, he had Jeb's friendship and his hope of losing himself in climbing was fulfilled.

Pete's thesis was titled *Human Cultivation and Dispersal of Economically Important Agricultural Products* and it chronicled the history of the human propagation of various plant species, over two dozen in total. The audience potentially interested in the in-depth academic topic was admittedly limited, but his work was not without a few fascinating histories. Pete pulled the copy from the bookshelf and re-read a section that he suddenly remembered to be relevant to his situation, hoping to better understand what he had gotten himself into.

"Humans have been enjoying, and most likely abusing, the narcotic effects of the poppy plant for over 5,000 years. The Sumerians were the first to document the plant, which they called *hul gil*, translating to *joy plant* in English. Since then, it and its derivatives have known many other names by many other cultures: *heart-pleasing*, *magical*, and *God's Own Medicine*.

From lower Mesopotamia, the cultivation and use of opium spread as quickly as traders could carry the seeds—Greece, Egypt, India, and eventually China. It was brought to China by European traders, and soon Britain wielded immense influence over China through the country's collective addiction. China sought to reduce their trade deficit and its citizens' dependence by blocking importation of opium, but the addiction was too great and the profits too high. The resulting Opium Wars of the 19th century were disastrous for China, ceding Hong Kong to Britain in addition to heavy retributions. These events are not unique in history; the poppy and its derivatives have long been used to control and enslave people, races, and countries. The U.S. government, in particular, has tried to use the poppy as a political tool, in some cases through the prohibition of its production and trade but in others as a method to finance opposition armies and rebels. This strategy failed in Vietnam and Afghanistan but will inevitably be tried again.

Chemists, as well as the philosophers and alchemists that explored the natural sciences before the term *chemist* came to be, have long sought to control the power of the plant, distilling it into other forms such as morphine, codeine, and heroin. But its power could not be controlled, and the distillates only served to increase human addiction and consequent destruction rather than subdue the plant into better-behaved intoxicants."

Reading this section made Pete further question his decision to join Jeb in trying to sell the heroin, joining the historical ranks of people profiting from other's addictions. Pete had never experimented with hard drugs before, and had no desire to, but he climbed and he couldn't help but to find them analogous. The mindlessness experienced during a climb—in a hard, bold lead, the rush of a big fall, the euphoria of a proud ascent—sensations hard to replicate in everyday life. That a higher high is always burdened by more serious consequences. That the single-minded pursuit of pleasure can lead one to become oblivious to many discomforts, uninterested in the security of relative wealth and long-term relationships, and discard most possessions along the way—except the kit and the van parked somewhere that nobody will bother. The sensation of lightness, whether induced by drugs or climbing, is a dangerous sensation to become dependent on. It usually happens right before a fall.

Chapter Eight

The hillside was too steep for Burl to navigate the thick sagebrush and loose limestone scree in his cowboy boots, so he walked back to his truck to grab his walking stick before making his way back to the edge of the road. He switchbacked down to the site where he'd found Lyle's body. It was his first time back to the scene since that night, but with the recent news of the gunshot wound, he needed to look around again.

The soil was still littered with broken glass and bits of plastic, and much of the dry grass was still noticeably disturbed. He'd already walked up and down the shoulder of the highway multiple times, only seeing an empty can of snuff, a trucker's piss bottle, and a few .22 shells, which he shoved in his pocket. He walked through the sage, using his walking stick to push the thin branches out of the way as he looked underneath. Up ahead, he saw blood on the dry cheatgrass. He walked toward it and then knelt, struck by emotion. Out of habit, Burl started to cross himself, hand moving from his head to chest, but he stopped before he could complete the motion. He closed his eyes, remembering the night he was last here.

Once the emotion had eased, Burl stood back up. He leaned onto his walking stick, a bit dizzy from the welling of feeling or maybe from standing too quickly. Burl looked around the site again as he regained his balance. A few footprints were still visible in the dirt—some cowboy boot tracks, undoubtedly his, and some lugged soles most likely from the EMTs' work boots. A bit further downhill, Burl saw a footprint that was different from the rest. He moved to a knee again to inspect closer. The print had a waffle pattern, flat without a heel or an arch, undoubtedly left by a sandal—or a flip-flop.

***

Jeb held the Econoline steady as the high-plains Wyoming wind tried its best to blow it off the road. Pete had his feet up on the dash and was gazing out the window. "Whatcha staring at, Pete?" Jeb said, breaking Pete's daydream. "Those soybeans?"

Pete shook his head. "Those are sugar beets, numbnuts. And I wasn't staring, I was thinking. You should try it sometime."

"Sugar beets? What the fuck are they?"

Pete picked up his thesis from the dash and thumbed through it, then began to read.

"The ancestor of the modern sugar beet is the wild sea beet, native to the coastlines of Europe, Africa and Asia. Due to the sea beet's indigenous soil being close to the ocean, they and their relatives have a high tolerance for sodium and can be grown in high alkaline soil where many other crops cannot. The distillation of juice from a common red beet into a syrupy sugar was first described in the 1500's. The result wasn't as flavorful as commonly available cane sugar..."

Pete was interrupted by the sound of the van's engine sputtering loudly. They looked at each other with concern as Jeb steered the shuddering van to the shoulder.

"Damn, Jeb, did we run out of gas again?"

Jeb shut off the van and unbuckled his seatbelt. "Not this time, Skinny. Tank shows half full and the check engine light is on." Jeb pulled the lever to unlatch the hood, then got out to take a look. Living in a van, especially an Econoline or worse a VW, usually comes with an honorary degree in mechanics, and Jeb had become an adept student. He became lost in the engine compartment, with only occasional cursing to let Pete know he was still there.

"Give 'er a go!" yelled Jeb after a few more minutes fiddling. Pete slid into the driver's seat and turned the key. The engine sputtered again.

"Damn it. Sounds like a bad coil, maybe a bad plug. It's definitely missing on a cylinder," Jeb said, wiping some sweat from his forehead. "Hopefully that's all it is. Hate to think what else it could be. We could hitch back to Worland or into Thermopolis and try to catch a Napa or Autozone before they close."

Pete looked around, concerned. They weren't in the middle of nowhere, but they might have been near one of its edges. Green beet stalks bordered the road on both sides, but beyond the fields stretched stark Wyoming desert until the rugged Bighorn mountains jutted up 60 miles to the east. They'd passed a trailer house a few miles previous but hadn't seen another vehicle since Worland.

"We can't leave the van just sitting here, considering its contents and all," Pete said. "Maybe you should go, and I'll stay here and watch the van. Or we could tow it to town, I guess."

Jeb dug in the glovebox for his wallet and grabbed his railroad cap from the floor. "No, I'll go. I don't want to flat tow this thing with the tranny problems we had down at Hueco. Best if I go solo and you play guard. Shouldn't take me too long." Jeb tucked his long tangles of hair underneath his cap, figuring it would improve his chances of getting picked up.

Despite the lack of traffic, Jeb thought the odds of getting a ride were good, as while hitchhiking as a Western tradition was disappearing as quickly as two-finger steering wheel waves and drive-through liquor stores, Wyoming seemed to be the last bastion for all three. Generations ago, hitching was almost a recreational activity, but somewhere between the changing mores and made-up stories of grisly murders, it was relegated to an act of desperate necessity. Jeb was too young to remember those days, but he did feel oddly liberated as he put out his thumb at a passing pickup.

Ten minutes passed before another car approached, which motored by without even a wave. As Jeb was finishing his second cigarette, an old blue Chevy pickup slowed down and pulled over to the shoulder of the road behind the van. Jeb ran up to the passenger door as the driver leaned over to roll the window down. He was a grey-haired man, wearing a frayed Western shirt and oil-spotted felt cowboy hat.

"Howdy. You fellers need some help, or a ride?" The man's walrus mustache bounced as he spoke.

"I could use a ride, if you could," said Jeb. "Where you headed?"

"The mighty metropolis of Thermopolis," the driver said, winking.

"Is there a car parts store there?"

"You bet. Couple of 'em, in fact. Get on in. Name's Gordon," he said, reaching a hand over to Jeb. Between his drawl and the bushy mustache hiding his lips, Jeb was struggling to understand him.

"I'm Jeb. Nice to meet ya. Thanks for the lift."

"Where you headed? I mean, once that orange hunk of shit is running again, that is." Gordon laughed. He put the truck in gear and pulled back onto the highway, waving to Pete as he passed by the parked van.

"We're on our way up to Canada, sir. Squamish. Been climbing in Ten Sleep for a few months now, but the heat is started to wear on us. No real plans yet, seeing where we end up. We're heading up to the Tetons now. Never been there."

"Ah, the ol' Jackson Hole. Mighty pretty. You rock climbers seem to be a mobile sort. Can't figure out when y'all find the time to work. What's wrong with your rig?"

"I think it's just a coil or a plug," Jeb replied.

"Is that a 351 in that thing? If so, my money would be on the coil. Them pieces of shit don't seem to last for long." Gordon laughed a bit maliciously, as if he was glad it was Jeb's problem and not his.

"I don't know. Outside of a little coolant leak, it has been running pretty good for a long time. Goes through a lot of antifreeze though. Are you a mechanic?"

"No, but I've turned a fair share of wrenches in my time. I run the sugar beet mill up in Worland. Always something breaking down, ya know. On top of the fleet of shitty old trucks at the mill, we got beet elevators, washers, shredders, evaporators. You name it, if it's been at the mill it's been broken. My job is keeping it all running. As my ex-wife used to tell me, if you can't be handsome, you better be handy." Gordon's laugh sounded as much like a cough as laughter.

The road was perfectly straight for as far as they could see, which relieved Jeb as Gordon didn't seem to be paying much attention to the highway. Out the window, the rhythmic motion of a pump jack in the distance syncopated with the pulsating of irrigation sprinklers. Jeb got temporarily lost in thought.

"Sugar beets? What are they?" asked Jeb, suddenly experiencing déjà vu. Gordon chuckled again and started unraveling the layers in the strange history of the sugar beet.

***

Jeb arose from his stupor, blinking his eyes rapidly. The story of beets had been too dull for him to stay mindful, his thoughts bouncing randomly from climbing, cooking, and past girlfriends.

He looked out the window at the large mineral feature that marked the north edge of the town of Thermopolis.

"So, where is it?" Gordon demanded, looking intently at Jeb. The question startled Jeb, whose thoughts were still back in time. Suddenly he was awake and remembering the box that Pete was guarding.

"Where is what?"

Gordon didn't avert his gaze. Jeb slowly moved his hand to the door handle, drawing his shoulders up with tension.

"Where is it that you are from?" Gordon replied, frustrated at having to ask again.

"Oh," Jeb said, relieved. "Kentucky. A little town called Owingsville, on the I-64 corridor."

"Hmm, a *corn cracker*. Should have guessed that from the accent."

"What about you?" asked Jeb.

"Me? I'm from nowhere, really. Been bouncing around from the day I was born. Pennsylvania, Iowa, Nevada, hell, even Washington state. I've been just about anything you can think of, too—trucker, welder, ranch hand. Now I'm a gad-damned beet juicer."

Gordon pulled the truck into the parking lot shared between a bakery and auto parts store. "Here you go, buddy. Good luck with your van."

Jeb opened the truck door and stepped out. "Thanks for the lift. I really appreciate it." He leaned back into the truck and extended his hand to Gordon.

"Grab a bottle of *KT's Leak Stop* while you are in there. Pour it in the radiator and run the heat for an hour or so. Only stops the leak 'bout half the time but it might save you from puttin' in a new one."

"Thanks, will do." Jeb closed the truck door and started towards the entrance before hearing Gordon shout at him through the truck's open window.

"Tell you what—I'll swing back by in few minutes and give ya a lift back out there. As a Chevy guy, I get a special thrill out of a broke-down Ford."

CHAPTER NINE

Burl quit smoking years ago, around the time he committed to drinking less, but if there was a time that he would take a cigarette if offered, it was now. Lyle's funeral had affected him much more than he had thought, and while he knew he would regret a cigarette later, he thought the nicotine would temporarily distract him from his grief. He was a friend of Lyle's, and his personal involvement in the case made him feel more emotionally connected. He knew it should be the other way around, *professional detachment* it was called, but he didn't really care. He was too old, and at the moment, too emotional. He sat in his truck alone, making the short drive from the Worland cemetery to the Two Bit Saloon where Sunny was hosting a reception to celebrate Lyle's life. Burl knew the bar would be full of people and he didn't feel much like socializing—he preferred grieving in solitude. He drove slowly, windows down, thinking about the fishing trip he and Lyle took to Yellowtail reservoir years ago. The outboard had broken down as they navigated a side canyon, leaving the pair stranded for hours while they waited for another boat to pass through. They caught a few fish and drank all the beer in the cooler before another boat finally towed them back to dock. Lyle was a reserved man, as was Burl, and the time spent drifting on the boat was one of the few times the two of them had ever really talked about anything other than fishing, history, or the weather. Burl blathered his life's regrets, mainly leaving a smaller impact on the world than he once dreamt, while Lyle spoke about his love for Sunny and his dream of taking her to see the ocean someday.

Burl started singing the refrain from the *Streets of Laredo*, which was stuck in his head after Lyle's uncle had sung it at the service. It was one of Burl's favorite cowboy ballads, a song that he found tremendously sad even before he associated it with Lyle. Now the words were making his eyes well with tears.

Please, beat the drum slowly and play the fife lowly
Play the Death March as you carry me along
Take me to the green valley, there lay the sod o'er me
For I'm a young cowboy and I know I've done wrong

Burl hadn't really paid attention to the words since he first learned the song as a boy, but now, singing to himself, he parsed them carefully. As he slowly drove down Highway 16 over the Nowood River into town, he wondered if Lyle had shared the young Laredo cowboy's guilt.

***

Burl stood in the back corner of the saloon drinking a Budweiser, trying to avoid talking to anyone. The bar was almost full, most everyone a local friend of Lyle's although there were a few people that Burl did not recognize, whom he assumed to be out-of-town friends or family. Still, Burl did not feel social and certainly didn't want to talk about Lyle. He pretended to admire the rattlesnake skin pinned to the wooden wall above the window, a small handwritten plaque hanging below it stating *Dry Creek, 1993*. He still remembered the day that Mike Steward killed that snake and brought the skin into the bar, claiming it to be the biggest ever found in the county. Burl smiled as he remembered the drunken discussion that followed, thinking back to happier and simpler days. As his gaze shifted from the wall back to the bar, he met eyes with Sunny. He quickly broke eye contact—she was the last person he wanted to talk to. Burl preferred his emotions simple and singular.

Sunny walked away from the woman with whom she had been talking, then back behind the bar. She disappeared under the bar momentarily, arising with a wooden box clutched in her hands. She walked toward Burl, pausing briefly as she looked over her shoulder.

"Hi, Burl," she said softly. He stepped closer to give her a hug before he noticed the case she was holding. "Can I talk to you outside for a second?"

Burl nodded and followed her out the front door. As is typical for an evening in Ten Sleep, the streets and sidewalks were empty.

"I am sorry I didn't call you earlier, Sunny. I am so sorry about Lyle. Just didn't quite know what to say."

"It's OK, Burl. I understand." Sunny presented the case to Burl. "Lyle would've wanted you to have this. He really admired you, you know."

Burl looked at the case confused. He couldn't think of any of Lyle's possessions that would have any meaning to him. "What is it?" he asked as he flipped open the small brass closure. Inside was a long, chipped-rock spearpoint, matte-grey in color.

"His Folsom point?" Burl looked surprised. "You should keep this. Or at least sell it to help cover some debts. It's worth a mint, you know."

Sunny shook her head. "It's yours. Please. Lyle loved the time he spent out hunting points with you. He always came back exhausted, but happy, even when y'all didn't find anything." She smiled weakly at Burl.

"I didn't really do much hunting, to be fair. Lyle did most of the work. I just drove him on the four-wheeler, anywhere he wanted to go. Might have opened a few gates for him along the way as well, but that's all the credit I can take. Lyle had a good eye, always knew where to look. I remember the day we found this one—high up on the plateau by Cloud Peak."

"He talked a lot about that spot. Told me he wanted to take me there soon, had a surprise for me. Can't imagine what it could've been."

Burl and Sunny met eyes in silence. Sunny pursed her lips as if she wanted to say more, but then stepped forward and gave him a hug. "Take care of yourself," she said before walking back inside, leaving Burl standing outside alone in the dark.

CHAPTER TEN

"Ever put gochujang on a peanut butter sandwich? It's fucking delicious," said Jeb with a mouth full of food. "I'll make you one if you want."

"Go choo jang?," asked Pete from the passenger seat. "What the fuck is that?"

"Gochujang. It's fermented chili paste from Korea. I picked up a jar at that natural food store we stopped at in Lander," said Jeb. "Where did you grow up, Montana? Uncultured redneck."

"Oh- this from a civilized and gallant gentleman such as yourself? I think the pot might be calling the kettle black."

Jeb laughed. "Speaking of pot, let's get another spliff rolling before we hit Jackson."

"Take it easy buddy. We've got a long way to go before Jackson. Let's make sure that new coil fixes everything before we start counting chickens."

"She's running as smooth as can be, Skinny. Maybe the leak-stop will even fix the radiator. That old man seemed to know his way around an engine compartment."

"How do you know about gochujang, anyway? Have you been to Korea?"

"Are you kidding? I've never left the country. I learned about gojuchang from some cooking shows I've been watching on my phone at night. Really good shit." Jeb stared out the windshield, trying to recall some of his favorite episodes. "France has their seven mother sauces, Korea has three—doenjang, ganjang, and gojuchang. And each one of them kicks the shit out of bechamel! Escoffier can eat a dick!" Jeb laughed, as if Pete was in on the joke.

Pete shook his head. "Never been out of the country? What about Canada, dumbass?"

"Canada doesn't count. They're just friendlier versions of ourselves. And apart from poutine, they eat the same stuff we do. I want to go somewhere *alien*. Korea would check that box—we should go there after we get our money."

"How about Vietnam instead? Let's go somewhere we can climb."

Jeb shook his head. "Korea is full of climbing. Yongseo Pokpo, Ganhyeon, Seonunsan—it's endless. Uncultured redneck."

Pete laughed. "Is that what you want to do with your share of the money—travel?"

"Yeah, maybe. Or upgrade the van and stick around the states. Haven't thought about it too much. You?"

"Not sure either. Maybe travel." Pete picked up a pair of clippers from the van's dash and started cutting his fingernails, the ends flying through the air. He hadn't let himself think much about the money yet as it made him nervous every time he did. A lot could still go wrong—not only in the deal with Dan, but with the problems that money created. Most of the world toiled to increase wealth, comfort, and possessions, but Jeb and Pete had pointed their compasses in the opposite direction, joining a subculture that competed to see who can survive on the least. Without the burden of mortgages, career objectives, or matching living room suites, they had a freedom that could never be purchased. He hoped any newfound wealth wouldn't compromise his ideals.

"How long do you think you could do this?" Pete asked.

"Do what?"

"Dirtbagging around the country. Working as little as possible, living on margins, climbing."

"I don't know. I guess I've never thought about it. Are you thinking of joining the real world? Not a fucking job, I hope."

"No, I'm just wondering. There has to be an end to this, right? I don't mean living in a van or climbing all the time. I mean living this...*free*. There has to be a reason everybody doesn't do it. At least not for long."

Jeb squinted, seeking to clarify his thoughts. "People don't do it because they don't know it's possible or how easy it is. We're taught as kids that security and comfort are the main goals in life. Those are opposite of freedom—all about money and order." Jeb was shaking his head, barely paying attention to the road. "We might not have security and comfort in excess at the moment, but I for one am having a pretty good time."

Pete stared straight. "Would you live this way if it didn't allow you to climb so much? Is it the freedom or the fun?"

"Both. No doubt about it. It's really a way of life—freedom and fun." Jeb looked proud of his righteousness.

"True," said Pete, "I think other people look at us and see all the shit we don't have that they can't imagine life without—retirement accounts, queen beds, underground sprinklers, whatever. But I look at them and see health insurance, a little money in the bank, not worrying about being able to pay the cell phone bill. Not exactly extravagances, but I wouldn't mind having them." Pete paused. "You ever think about those things?"

"Nope—never." Jeb turned to Pete to judge his reaction. "Of course I do, Skinny. And heavier shit even: What if my mom gets hurt and can't work? What if the van breaks down and we can't cover the repair costs? There are a million things that could interfere with my life, and I will deal with them as they arise." Pete wasn't sure what to say. Jeb seemed to brush off worry better than he did. "But you know what currently really worries me?" Jeb asked.

Pete shook his head, "No. What?"

"You leaving your fingernail clippings on the floor."

The van and its occupants continued westward, driving straight into the sun. The passenger window rolled down as a handful of fingernails flew out into the Wyoming wind.

Chapter Eleven

Dan grew up in the logging town of Gold River on the west coast of Vancouver Island. The son of a logger, his family fell on tough times when the local mill closed. As a result, he started to work young, first washing dishes in a diner but eventually replanting trees in the various clearcuts on the island and around western Canada. Dan discovered climbing while working in the forests near the giant granite domes of Squamish. It changed his life; giving him a community, a belief in experiences outside of himself, and a reason to explore the world. He went on expeditions in the Himalaya and Karakoram, pilgrimages to Patagonia and the Peruvian Andes, and climbed extensively through the Canadian Rockies. While he developed an appreciation for his work planting trees, his job was only a means to climb as much as possible.

Dan's experimentation with heroin in Thailand had turned into full-blown addiction upon returning to Vancouver. The habit was too expensive to maintain along with his extended vacations to climb, so climbing became the second casualty of his addiction, behind friends and family. Ultimately, he learned that even minor dealing was more lucrative than planting trees, and soon his recreation became his vocation, but not one without peril. Situations that Dan had considered dangerous a few years ago became acceptable and routine. As with climbing, danger can become normalized until the risks taken are no longer reasonable by any metric, usually so slowly that the process is imperceptible. Sometimes it takes a life-threatening event to reveal the accumulated risk; to renormalize back to reasonable levels—but often that event is either ignored or fatal.

Dan had started in the business by simply helping out his dealer in exchange for junk. Initially, he ran errands and washed cars. With trust, he started transporting cash and splitting up bricks. Soon he had his own customers and minor territory. Dan bought his supply at wholesale, split it up and kept the profits—a simple arrangement, and the risks were clear. It was also indentured servitude to addiction, with no obvious exit. Dan didn't question how his dealer was supplied, or to whom he was connected. Eventually, after years of this comfortable arrangement, Dan's dealer told him that he was up for *promotion* and made the introduction to his superiors in the Hóng Lóng Triad—the second largest Chinese organized crime syndicate in the world.

The Triad had established operations in Vancouver from their base in Hong Kong over a decade ago. Smuggling heroin and humans were their specialties, and Vancouver was an attractive port for both. The group operated similarly to other organized crime networks, covering their operation with bribes and payoffs, and controlling their ranks with violence and fear. A rival gang had been undermining their heroin sales, and they were eager to try to reclaim some territory. The new position for Dan, managing supply and collection with street dealers, came with more money, increased protection provided by the Triad, and a descent into organized crime. Risk was creeping up at nearly the rate it was being normalized. He had stopped climbing. He rarely smiled. He lost touch with his friends and climbing partners. Gravity was gone, but he had begun to fall.

***

Xin Li, the Mountain Master, was not entirely surprised at Chen's failure, but he wanted to appear so to keep the young Triad member nervous. Fear was an important tool for managing new recruits, known as *49ers* in the Triad hierarchy, and Xin Li was an expert in its use. He had been initiated into the Triads in Hong Kong before being relocated to Canada as the head Enforcer of the Vancouver chapter. He needed to prove his value to his superiors overseas.

He sat behind a metal desk in an otherwise empty room, wearing a black jacket over a black shirt, staring at Chen seated in front of him across a bare desk. "If you fail me again, I will be forced to discuss the matter with the Dragon Head. And Wang

Xiu is much less tolerant of failure than I." Xin Li flicked his cigarette ash onto the floor and took a long drag, which he blew towards Chen's face. Dramatic effect was another important tool in manipulating the workers.

"We need to recover our losses from the laowai called Dan. We cannot allow him to embarrass us any longer. I need you to collect our money. Then kill him." Xin Li stood up and left through the back door, his burning cigarette still smoking in the ashtray.

Xin Li's threats had been very convincing to Chen when he first was initiated into the gang but had been losing their effectiveness lately. Chen could see through the tenuous grip on power that he held and knew that Xin Li was losing respect with the other Enforcers as well. But Chen also knew that the consequences of failure were higher than he wanted to pay. He was tired of it all—the charades, the meaningless pedestal of honor, the constant violence and danger. Mostly, he was just tired.

Xin Li had brought Chen from Hong Kong to Vancouver five years ago, claiming that Chen's predecessor was retiring. Chen suspected that Xin Li had him killed, as weeks after his supposed retirement his mutilated body washed up in the Vancouver harbor. Chen knew he had little choice in the transfer and promotion, and as apprehensive as he was replacing a murdered member, he was excited to experience the western world. He had been first introduced to the American West through cowboy movies, fascinated by the contrast of the stark red deserts to the densely populated madness of Hong Kong. Chen identified with the cattle rustlers and train robbers that were often portrayed, wishing he was a maverick nomad instead of pawn in a game he no longer wanted to play.

Once Xin Li had left, Chen snubbed out the burning cigarette and slouched against the back of his chair. He pulled out his phone and flipped through recent photos of his new motorhome and its maiden voyage though the Icefields Parkway. It was too grand, he thought, to be called a van, even if it was built on a van chassis. Large enough to be comfortable, even luxurious, yet still small enough to maneuver and park. Black exterior, four-wheel drive, wood and leather interior—perfect. He couldn't wait to get on the road, for good this time, seeing the great open places of the world firsthand.

****

Dan looked at himself in the bathroom mirror in disbelief. It was a body and a face he recognized, but not one that he knew, as if looking at someone he hadn't seen for years. His beard mostly hid the hollowed cheeks and pale complexion, but there was something about his eyes that made him look away. During the moments in which he possessed enough clarity for honest reflection, he knew his current state was the direct result of a cascade of poor decisions. Bad luck couldn't be blamed—he had a good family, a happy childhood, and enough intelligence and skill to make a decent living. And he had climbing, a pursuit that gave him joy and a vision for the future. He had more than most.

There was a moment that still burned bright in Dan's memory, even though it happened over a decade ago. Dan was high on a chossy peak in the Canadian Rockies, runout 40 feet above his last piece of protection, his crampons skating on a featureless quartzite slab, his ice tools barely holding their purchase on narrow edges of rock. He debated climbing back down in hopes of finding a crack to place protection or barring that, retreating. Instead, he moved upward, making a move that he knew he couldn't reverse. He had fully committed, and now up was the only way to safety. Once he and his partner were safely back on flat ground, Dan vowed to never take such large chances again. From that moment forward, Dan's climbing became more methodical and controlled.

Now he'd lost control again, and the stakes were just as high. He wondered if another promise to himself could work. Dan dried off his hair, grateful for the short moment of lucidity a hot shower had granted. He got dressed and walked through the living room, his roommate Julian on the couch playing video games, unaware of his presence. Julian was a junkie too; Dan wondered if he looked as robotic as Julian did. He opened the front door and stepped into the last rays of the setting Vancouver sun. He took a deep breath. The oppression of his addiction was still heavy, but Dan could feel hope rising. It felt foreign yet familiar, like recognizing the face of a forgotten childhood friend. The feeling made him smile.

Jeb had called him that morning and pitched his proposition. It was an opportunity that could bring a peaceful end to his dealings with the Triads, motivation to find a new occupation, and some distance from his addiction. With enough resolve and the help of an old friend, maybe a new start was possible.

CHAPTER TWELVE

Seventy miles north of Ten Sleep, high on the Bighorn plateau, lies a mysterious circle of rocks known as the Medicine Wheel. Its origins and original purpose are unknown, perhaps reaching back a millennium, but regional tribes have used the site for centuries as a sacred place for prayer and vision quests. One such people are the Apsáalooke, commonly known as the Crow. They arrived in the greater Yellowstone region after being pushed west by the Sioux and Cheyenne tribes, only to be forced onto a government-created reservation centered on the Bighorn and Pryor mountains. The Crow tribe held both mountain ranges sacred and believed the Pryors to be occupied by the Nirumbee, or Little People. These small but fierce people were elusive and rarely seen, but the Crow believed that petroglyphs in the mountains were evidence of their long occupation in the Pryor mountains. The many stone arrowheads the Crow found in the area were also attributed to the Little People, as the Crow tribe did not *flintknap*, the process of creating stone hunting points by hand, and instead used bone for their arrow points.

The point that Burl was holding at his kitchen table was not made by the Crow nor the Little People, but most likely by a member of a nomadic tribe of mammoth hunters nearly ten millennia ago. Lyle and Burl had found it high on the Bighorn plateau, far above Ten Sleep canyon. Burl knew it was Lyle's most prized point, not only because of its rarity and the spectacular place that it was found, but also due to the physical connection this point had to a history he knew so little about. Even holding it in his hands, Burl felt a connection to its creator. His thumb flicked over the point's sharp edge as he imagined what its original owner might have been like. Burl wondered if he felt fear during his hunts, if he had ever pondered his own death, whether he felt the emotion of love. It seemed to Burl that he must have—what else would give him the strength and courage to survive the hardship and danger, or the motivation to overcome the fear that must have endlessly haunted his days? What keeps us alive except the fragile armistice between fear and love?

While Lyle did keep the exceptional point or scraper, it was more common that he left them as he found them or reburied them if he'd been digging or sifting. The notion had always confused Burl—what was the purpose of looking for points if not to collect them? Why hunt for them at all? Lyle had explained to him once: *It's like our own pasts, Burl. You gotta dig shit up and stare at it once in a while, even if you just plan on burying it again. Keeping it buried serves nothing.* Burl still didn't know if it made any sense. He had inhumed his trauma from Vietnam and the pain from his wife Mary's losing battle with cancer and saw no point in ever reflecting on them again.

Burl stood up and walked to his bedroom, kneeling down by the bottom dresser drawer. He slid it open and reached to the back, behind the neat folds of clothes that used to belong to his wife. He wasn't sure why he had kept them. Burl produced an orange prescription bottle with a few medical marijuana cigarettes inside, left over from his wife's chemotherapy sessions, now a decade old. He hadn't had one for years, but it seemed like the right occasion. He was ready to be done thinking for a while.

***

From his truck bed parked high on the mesa, Burl trained his binoculars on the storage sheds where Cole was working. He twirled the toothpick in his mouth with his tongue as he tried to piece together a theory. Burl couldn't get the missing horse out of his mind and was surprised that Cole hadn't shown more concern with its disappearance. Burl didn't believe that Cole's cutting horses were valuable enough to kill for, but he also couldn't believe that Cole hadn't tried harder to find it in the two weeks since it disappeared, with or without Burl's help. Lacking any other leads, and with not much else happening in Washakie county at the moment, Burl decided to watch Cole as closely as he could. So far, he had learned that the sergeant probably drank a bit too much, tended to his tomatoes in their hothouses regularly, and liked watching Sportscenter at night.

Burl was a part of a disappearing generation of old cowboys, ranchers and farmers whose beings were deeply intertwined with the land on which they lived. The younger generations were born into a smaller world and into a more mobile mindset, and as a result they weren't shaped as much by the place in which they lived. Burl thought that Cole held on to the old western ways more than most of his generation but wondered what Cole had meant when he'd said that the deserts of the Middle East had changed him.

Burl stared through the binoculars at a blue Chevy pulling into the driveway off the county road. The truck could have belonged to a half dozen people in the county; Burl struggled to resolve the driver's face. The Chevy rolled to stop next to Cole's truck and the driver got out.

"Hello Gordon," muttered Burl, finally seeing the man's face clearly. Gordon's mustache was unmistakable, even at distance. "What brings your charming self our way?" Burl twirled the toothpick again, pondering the connection between Gordon and Cole. In a town the size of Ten Sleep, Burl knew, or thought he knew, the friendships, work relationships, trysts, and animosities that webbed the place and people together. Gordon and Cole together didn't make sense.

Burl continued watching through his binoculars. The conversation between Cole and Gordon was animated. Burl could clearly see frustration, if not a bit of anger, on both men's faces. Gordon turned away as Cole lost his temper. He slammed his hand down on Gordon's truck, spat on the ground, and walked off. Gordon kicked the gravel and climbed back into his truck.

What are you boys up to? thought Burl, putting down his binoculars. He left his perch on the edge of the mesa and got back into his truck. He stared out the windshield at the desert valley below, trying to think of a relation between the two men, once again wishing he still smoked, as sometimes the distraction of smoking allowed his mind to wander to places it was otherwise confined from. *Perhaps another cup of coffee will help*, he thought as he started up his truck and slowly drove back into town.

***

The Bighorn Cafe served weak coffee and spongey eggs, but Burl found both close to perfection. One benefit of not being particularly worldly was that he wasn't very particular. The Cafe used to be a busy place in the mornings when the local farmers and ranchers would get together to trade stories and gossip over biscuits and gravy. It had always been a good place for Burl to connect to the community and stay current with county happenings, but the Cafe was much quieter these days and the younger generation didn't trust law enforcement enough to confide in him anyway. Still, it was a good place to think.

"Morning, Burl. Glad I ran into you. I've been meaning to talk to you," said Jim McDowell, another Café patron who was making his way past Burl's seat at the bar. Jim's legs looked comically skinny underneath his potato-like gut.

"Hey, Jim," said Burl, extending his hand. "Good to see you."

"Sorry I didn't get a hold of you earlier, been pretty busy at the ranch," Jim said, claiming a stool next to Burl. "I heard from Roger the other day that you had some suspicions about Lyle's death."

Burl's smile disappeared. "Perhaps. Can't say I've made much progress. Do you know something that might help?"

"Maybe, maybe not," Jim frowned. "I saw a truck parked in front of his house once this summer. Colorado plates, 90's Dodge with lots of chrome, a guy in the cab I didn't recognize. I never see anyone over at their place, so I guess it stood out a little to me. Even Sunny's rig is hardly ever there anymore." Jim glanced at Burl to see if he reacted. Burl nodded slowly. "Living nearby, you know. I'm not spying on them or anything, but you just can't help but to notice things."

"I understand, Jim. Is there anything else you can remember about the truck?"

"It had a sticker on the back window of a severed hand, middle finger up—cartoon-like. Said *Satan's Fingers* under it, if I remember right. Just odd enough to stick in my head, I guess. I'll let you know if anything else comes to mind. Hope it helps, really a shame about Lyle. He was a good man."

"I appreciate the help, Jim." Burl stood up to shake Jim's hand.

Burl turned back to his cold coffee and eggs. "Hey Rita, could I talk you into a warm up on the coffee?" he shouted down the bar. Between Cole, Gordon, Sunny's possible lover Monty, and a few strange footprints at the crime scene, he had a lot to think about.

***

Cole unlocked the door of the northwest greenhouse for his morning walkthrough. The hydrothermal heating system continued to produce incredible results, as evidenced by his current crop. Cole's father Roy had engineered a great environment for growing tomatoes, and Cole had refined it further for its current use. Row after row of plants stood tall in hydroponic planters, the green bulbs on the ends of their stalks looking as if they were about to burst, all illuminated by violet-hued LEDs. The air was warm and humid and had the smell of wet soil and chemical fertilizer.

Cole's time in Afghanistan had changed him. It had stolen his youth and his spirit, replacing them fear and hate. The every-day patrols and gunfights were the beginning of the erosion, but soon the count of dead friends, dead mothers, and dead children cemented the transformation of his previous calm to rage. Cole's squad conducted a raid based on bad intelligence that resulted in the deaths of an entire civilian family, and his trauma became more than he could handle on his own. Opium was readily available to troops in the region and provided brief respite from his pain. The production of opium in Afghanistan was viewed by the generals as a stabilizing force in an area with little stability. Troops were assigned occasional patrols of the fields and production facilities to limit, but also safeguard, production. Stability in the region required a carefully metered market. These patrols introduced Cole to the cultivation and production practices of making opium. At the time, he couldn't have imagined his occasional opium use would ever become habit, nor that his peripheral knowledge of poppy production would ever be useful.

When Cole returned home after his 15-month tour, he was granted a discharge and took over the tomato operation from his ailing father. A few poppies planted next to the tomatoes helped Cole blur his memories and temper the pain. The tomato operation was financially viable and could have provided Cole with enough income to be comfortable, as it had for his father before. But he felt he deserved something in return for the demons he had acquired during the war, and getting rich from growing poppies struck him as appropriately poetic.

Between the four greenhouses, Cole had over an acre of production space. Modern hydroponic techniques and grow-lamps, along with year-around heat from the hydrothermal system, allowed his operation to quickly outpace his supply chain and purification techniques. Poppies were easier to care for than tomatoes, and much more tolerant, and Cole was a proficient gardener after spending most of his teenage years in greenhouses working for his dad. Refinement of the opium into morphine had been simple enough for Cole to learn and manage on the farm, but the market demanded the purer, stronger refinement of heroin. This was outside of the knowledge and equipment available to Cole. But he suspected that it couldn't be any harder than making white sugar out of red beets and knew that Gordon Philips made a living doing exactly that.

CHAPTER THIRTEEN

"Pretty nice spot for lunch, hey brother?" Jeb said to Pete over the rushing wind. The pair sat on an expansive ledge known as the Grandstand—a wide, flat ridge of rock between the summit of Mount Owen to the north and the Grand Teton to the south. The cliff in front of them dropped two thousand feet down to the Teton glacier, behind them were the plains of Idaho and the distant Salmon River mountain range. To their right was the legendary North Ridge of the Grand Teton, a climbing route drenched in history and lore but of only moderate difficulty by modern standards.

His mouth full of sandwich, Pete could only manage a "Ymmph" and a thumbs up. Pete and Jeb had summited the nearby mountain Teewinot just as the sun was rising after a strenuous three hours in the dark, then traversed the long ridge between Teewinot and Owen's summit. The North Ridge stood between them and their third and final summit of the day, the Grand Teton. This link up is known to climbers as the Cathedral Traverse, named for the resemblance the three peaks have to cathedral towers. To most climbers, the spiritual overtone of the name is fully understood, but in different terms than most of the church-going crowd. The mountains are the temples—freedom, adventure, presence, and clarity are the creeds.

"Guess we find out now whether we should've brought a rope," laughed Jeb, looking up at the ridge above. The pair had decided to eschew the rope in order to save weight and move faster, but the decision inherently increased the risk. The pair knew from the guidebook that the climbing shouldn't challenge their abilities, but neither had been on this side of the Grand before or knew much about the escape if the climbing proved too dangerous or difficult. A rope would also make an emergency descent much easier in the event of bad weather or an accident.

"Safer this than smuggling drugs into Canada, right?" Pete said, smirking.

"Yeah. Overlooked that part of the plan, I suppose. We will figure something out, don't worry. How hard can it be to sneak a small package past a few friendly Mounties?"

If either Pete or Jeb were nervous about the climb, it didn't show. Pete, being a bit older and more experienced than Jeb, prided himself on his ability to process risk rationally—or at least as rationally as possible for the prejudiced human mind. Jeb hadn't reflected much on risk evaluation, his youthful confidence masking his lack of knowledge and experience. Perhaps arrogance, ignorance and bravery are all subtle shades of the same thing.

"You want to go first or second?" asked Jeb. He had spent lunch staring at the photocopied topo map of the Italian Cracks, the name of the feature the pair were to ascend up the ridge. "I think I got the topo wired if you want me to go first." Jeb couldn't contain his enthusiasm.

"Sure, sounds good. I'll give you a hundred feet and follow behind," said Pete, taking one more sip from his water bottle.

Jeb set off the up ridge, followed by Pete. The pair climbed quickly through the initial pitches to the point where the ridge steepened, using the many knobby features for purchase as well as jamming their hands and feet into the abundant cracks in the granite. Jeb paused before pulling himself onto a steep bulge, looking down to position his feet on the largest features he could find. He reached up high above his head blindly, finding a large block of rock to use as a handhold. He committed his weight to the block, moving his feet higher up to the next stance, only to feel the block shift in his hand. It broke free and slid toward him. He ducked, the block narrowly missing his head but falling directly toward Pete below.

"Rock!" yelled Jeb, steadying himself with his other hand while he watched the block fall within feet of Pete and explode on a rock shelf a hundred meters below. "Sorry!" Jeb kept climbing until he reached a ledge big enough to sit down on, waiting for Pete to catch up.

"Cool, man. Nice job. Pretty airy exposure, huh?" said Jeb, raising his palm for a high five.

"Dude...amazing," Pete replied, slapping Jeb's hand. "Careful with the loose rock, trying to kill me? I'll go first through this next bit."

Pete scrambled up the ledge to its apex, then onto the steeper face above, moving smoothly and efficiently. As Jeb waited his turn, he watched the thin swirling clouds above, seemingly building and getting darker. Jeb and Pete had planned to be off the summit before the afternoon due to the ever-present threat of thunderstorms, but perhaps they should have looked at the weather forecast more closely.

Pete studied the headwall above him as the climbing became more difficult, knowing that a slip here would be serious. He down-climbed to a comfortable position to wait for Jeb.

"Bust out that topo when you get up here," Pete said as Jeb approached. "Not sure where we are. The pitch above gets pretty steep."

The two huddled together on a narrow rib of rock and studied the topo, leaning their backs against the rock wall for security. "Looks like we might have blown past the traverse off of Second Ledge already," said Jeb. "I think this is Third Ledge. That must be the Pendulum Pitch above us, from the topo anyway." Jeb pointed to the spot on the map where he thought they were. "We either climb it or try to traverse out right off of this ledge and back on route."

Pete and Jeb studied the terrain above and to their right, imagining the individual moves necessary for each option. The holds on the pitch above looked insecure—Pete replayed the image of the rock Jeb pulled off detonating below him and shuddered.

"I don't know. The Pendulum Pitch looks pretty hard for 5.8. Not sure I want to solo that in my approach shoes. Don't really feel like down-climbing that last bit either. I guess the traverse out right?" Pete shrugged his shoulders and looked at Jeb, who shrugged back and started traversing right into the steep corner. After 10 meters of scrambling, he made a strenuous move into the corner crack, wedging his left fist into the fissure and reached blindly around the edge, hoping to find a good hold for his right hand. With a small grunt, he disappeared around the corner.

"Pretty sketchy, Pete! Be careful!" shouted Jeb from the other side. "Looks chill to the summit though."

Pete started across, using the same hand-jam as Jeb. It wasn't as secure as Jeb had made it look. He groped around the corner, finding only a small, slippery handhold. The north face of the Grand receives very little sunshine, and although his fingers were cold enough to start to lose feeling, Pete's hands were sweating. He had decided not to bring a chalkbag to save weight, so he wiped his hand on his pantleg to dry the sweat from his fingertips. He crimped onto the marginal hold as he smeared his left foot on the wall. As Pete tried to stab his right foot around the corner to a large ledge, his hand jam slipped, causing his tenuous foot-smear to come off its purchase. His body was weightless, time slowed to a stop. Without conscious thought, his right shoulder locked into position and his forearm flexed heavily as his entire weight loaded onto just three fingers, which were slowly sliding off a feature no bigger than the width of a pencil.

Pete's crimp held as his feet stopped slipping down the rock face. He jabbed a foot up to a ledge and found a larger hold for his left hand. Pete rocked up onto his feet to a safe stance next to Jeb. Pete's expression was blank. Jeb's eyes were wide with disbelief.

"Whoa, dude. Told you that was sketchy!" laughed Jeb, holding his hand out for a high-five. But Pete didn't laugh, nor slap Jeb's hand. He looked upward at the remaining distance to the summit and started climbing again.

Risk. Pete couldn't get the word out of his head. He kept climbing upwards, trying to quiet his mind, but the voice only seemed to get louder. *Risk.* He paused, speaking to himself to try to chase the voice away. *Reward.* But the voice returned. *Injury. Death.* He pushed back. *Clarity. Joy.* Pete saw Jeb approaching from below and started climbing again. *Is the risk worth the reward?* Pete moved faster. *Definitely.* His foot skated off a rock edge in his haste. *Maybe.*

Pete's mind had shifted to the package of heroin sitting in the van a mile below him. *Prison. Death.* He answered back: *Money. Freedom.* He was moving recklessly fast, but the voice was even louder than his hurried breaths. *Is it worth it?*

Pete didn't want to try to answer the question this time. He turned his mind to Lydia, hoping to reset. The voice pursued. *Vulnerability. Rejection.* He took a deep breath and returned the volley. *Acceptance. Love.* He was near the summit, trying to outrace his thoughts. He flowed over the last vertical face, scrambling through the boulders perched on top. He stepped onto the summit block and exhaled.

***

The summit of the Grand Teton is as spectacular as one would hope it would be while contemplating it from the valley floor. Its narrow platform drops dramatically off on all sides, but most impressively to the eastern valley floor some 6,000 feet below. For over a century, successful suitors of the Grand have sat at this spot, celebrating their ascent, soaking in the beauty of the range as seen from its highest summit, or contemplating their place in the natural world. Pete and Jeb, finding themselves alone on the summit, were crouched low behind a rock, smoking weed from an improvised pipe made from an apple core.

"Hey man, really sorry about what happened back there," said Pete, passing the makeshift pipe to Jeb.

"No worries, man. Hardly even smelt it."

Pete laughed. "No, I mean when my feet slipped. It was careless, shouldn't have happened," Pete said, looking at Jeb sincerely. "Sorry."

"Hey, part of the game, right?" Jeb said, taking a drag.

"I don't know—should it be?" Pete was staring out in the distance, asking the question to himself as much as Jeb.

Jeb shrugged. "Maybe, maybe not. Depends on what you are in it for I guess."

"I'm not in it to die, I know that much. I don't want to die climbing, Jeb. Seems so…" Pete paused, then looked back over at Jeb. "…selfish."

Jeb raised his eyebrows and sighed. "Climbing is selfish whether you die doing it or not. You do it because it makes you happy, right? Kind of the definition of selfishness, I would say. If you are worried about *looking* selfish, don't you think your friends and family just want you to be happy? Do you think they would grieve less if you died of cancer or got hit by a car? I wouldn't worry about appearing selfish. They know you for the great human being you are." Jeb looked directly at Pete. "It's not selfish to live on your own terms. It's your life to live." He exhaled loudly. "Want any more of this?" he asked, offering the apple pipe back to Pete.

"Nah, I'm good," Pete answered. His expression was blank as he considered Jeb's words.

Jeb stood up, and with surprisingly good form, wound up and threw the apple off the east face of the Grand Teton.

***

Jeb was tightening the laces of his approach shoes, preparing to start the long descent down the south side of the Grand Teton, but Pete wasn't yet ready to go. He leaned his head against the rock serving as his backrest and stared across Teton Valley. He replayed his carelessness a few more times before his mind started to wander. He wondered if he could find the activities of youth fulfilling again, or if climbing had led him down a one-way path that rendered normal pastimes pale. He had enjoyed pinball as a kid, but would he willfully risk his life to play—a choice he made without question with climbing. Imagine if the pinball machine electrocuted the player after too many mistakes? Or a game of bowling in which gutter balls were hurled back toward the bowler? Climbing wasn't always fun for Pete, often it was as many parts suffering. It was a complex experience combining the joy of movement, focus and concentration, and dedication to the immediate moment. It could generate thought so singular that his mind and body merged—or disappeared altogether. Yet somehow in this disappearance, Pete found that the subtle sensation of living could not be ignored—rare experience in modern life. Living so pure that risking death for it seems obvious.

Pete had long thought that the cliché of someone dying while doing what they loved was short-sighted. It placed the importance on the moment of death while trivializing the more important notion that the person lived consciously and with enough passion to pursue activities that they loved—despite of potential dangers. He closed his eyes and tried to convince himself that this was true; that the joy and richness that climbing brought him was worth the risks he encountered as collateral. He smiled as he then wondered if a person could readily die at an office job, shopping at a box store, or standing in line for a latte, that they might contemplate if they are really living the life that they want to.

Chapter Fourteen

Pete and Jeb and the orange Econoline cruised through Idaho's Snake River valley at a rate inflated by coffee but moderated by weed, resulting in a speed safe from any highway trooper's radar gun. The road ran straight and flat through immense sections of desert prairie, and outside of the leaking radiator the van was running great.

"The blind mule!" exclaimed Jeb, breaking the last hour's silence.

Pete squinted and looked over at Jeb. "What?"

"It's how we get the stash across the border. Last time I crossed the border going to Squamish they tore my car apart. We can't risk that. The blind mule solves all of that. Remember the story that Big Mike told us about flying through Singapore on his way back from Arapiles? Smugglers will sneak drugs in your bag at the airport when you are not looking and try to retrieve them without you knowing after customs. But if you get caught..." Jeb slid his hand across his throat. "Busted!" he said as he stuck his tongue out.

"Mike said he was so paranoid that he emptied his entire bag out on the floor of the airport before he got on the plane, dirty clothes and all." Pete laughed. "So what's a blind mule?"

"The blind mule doesn't know they are smuggling anything, an unwitting drug runner. Not only are the real runners safe, the mule is calm and cool and doesn't show the nervousness that give most away. We find a logging truck or something near the border. Maybe at a quieter crossing than Vancouver. Then we hide the package on the truck, follow it across the border, and grab it later," said Jeb, thinking his way through the plan as he spoke. "There's zero risk."

"I'd feel pretty bad if the trucker got caught with our stash," said Pete. "Not sure I like it."

"Agreed. But those logging trucks cross that border all the time. The guards probably even know the drivers' names. The chances of them getting busted is pretty low." Jeb smiled as an idea came to him. "We write a note explaining that the trucker doesn't know about the drugs, that a dangerous but conscientious drug gang is responsible, blah blah blah. Stick it in with the package. I think with enough detail the guards would believe it."

Pete pondered the idea. It certainly wasn't Jeb's worst idea, and Pete had been witness to many. "So, if you're so sure the guards will really believe a note excusing the mule, why don't we just be the mule ourselves? We write a note for *ourselves*. The *double* blind mule." Both Jeb and Pete laughed at the preposterous thought.

If ancient Persians really did debate ideas both sober and drunk to fully understand their merit, Jeb and Pete might have considered following up their slightly intoxicated discussion with a sober one. Instead, Pete started drafting a note.

***

The sagebrush gave way to pine trees as Pete and Jeb made their way further west. A short detour to Idaho and the granite spires of the City of Rocks to climb a few of the classic cracks, a couple of pee breaks, and a few stops for gas found the pair outside of Snoqualmie, Washington. The floor of the van was littered with potato chip bags and empty Yoo-hoo bottles, Black Sabbath's "Paranoid" was blasting from the speakers, and Pete was asleep and dreaming in the passenger seat.

Lydia's red hair was tangled around her helmet's straps, the remainder held back in a braid. Her freckles seemed especially pronounced in the soft afternoon light.

You're beautiful, Pete tried to speak telepathically to Lydia as their eyes met. Their legs hung over a granite ledge, looking out over the wind-riffled waters of the Howe sound. Pete put his hand on her knee as she laughed about Pete's poor climbing performance on the pitch before.

"Pretty fucking ragged, Petey! What were you doing up there, eh?" laughed Lydia, her Canadian accent sounding particularly strong.

"You looked like a monkey fucking a goddamn football!"

"Ha, yeah," said Pete. "I got my knee stuck for a bit and had to use my hips to wiggle my knee out." He was embarrassed. He wasn't sure he had trusted anyone as much before and was confused as to what it meant. He couldn't tell whether Lydia trusted, or loved, him as much.

"Hence the monkey/football thing, right?" said Lydia. "Really giving that crack the business. It was making me a bit jealous, ya know," Lydia laughed. "You're a dirty man, Petey boy."

"Stop it," said Pete, blushing. "You get to lead that pitch next time, then I can make fun of you." He smiled and gazed again at Lydia.

"If I wanted to rub my thighs against something hard I would-" Lydia cut herself off, as Pete was clearly uncomfortable with her vulgarity. "Sorry," she said as she punched Pete in the arm, "just giving ya grief, eh."

Pete blushed more and looked away. "Where to next?" he asked.

"Down—where else is there?" said Lydia, punching him on the shoulder again. She stood up and started preparing the rope for the rappels.

No, *thought Pete.* Where are WE going next. *He once again tried to telegraph his thoughts to Lydia.*

Lydia looked back at him as if she received his thought.

"C'mon," she said, "that beer down there ain't going to drink itself."

Pete was awakened from his sleep suddenly by the motion of the van swerving radically.

"Peeete!" screamed Jeb loudly, still rocking the steering wheel back and forth.

Pete braced for impact, but the van quickly straightened out and resumed its course on the highway. He looked out the side window but saw nothing that might have caused the commotion. He stared over at Jeb, confused.

"Knock it off. You were farting in your sleep again."

Pete held his gaze, anger boiling. "Killing both of us is an interesting solution to a couple of farts."

Jeb turned up the Sabbath and pretended to have not heard Pete. Pete closed his eyes again, hoping to return to his dream of Lydia.

Chapter Fifteen

The Worland Sugar Company was a busy place near the end of the summer, as the plant needed to be ready to accept beet deliveries immediately following the first frost of the fall. It was a time of year that Gordon typically looked forward to, but right now he didn't need any additional stress. He was standing on a ladder rinsing out one of the evaporator tanks as a diversion from thinking about his current problems. It was a menial job, one that he would normally hand off to one of his employees, but at the moment it cleansed his mind along with the tank.

As much as Gordon didn't initially believe Cole, the sugar plant was indeed the perfect facility for processing opium. The evaporators, mixers, boilers, granulators and filters all had their roles. It was a simple process, and while Gordon didn't necessarily understand all the chemistry involved, he was diligent, clean, and careful. The final purification step was the only dangerous one, as a small mistake could result in a violent explosion. Gordon always made Cole come to the plant to conduct it himself. Otherwise, Gordon handled production on his own, usually after the sugar crews had left for the evening or on weekends during the slower months.

Along with having access to the equipment, Gordon's connections in the food processing industry allowed him to purchase the necessary bulk chemicals that would otherwise raise flags with the DEA. The procurement of these materials was the riskiest aspect of the process, outside of the risk in the end distribution, of course, from which Cole promised Gordon was fully shielded. Between his access to the sugar plant's equipment and his ability to procure the essential chemicals, Gordon realized that he probably had the upper hand in his business relationship with Cole. However, Cole's forceful personality easily overpowered Gordon's, so now Cole's missing heroin problem was suddenly his.

Getting into business with Cole was a winding path and one that Gordon was still not certain about. The legal consequences were obvious, but it was Cole's temper that concerned him more—once in their early experimentations in refinement, Gordon had ruined a batch of brew with an incorrectly set timer, causing Cole to shoot holes into the smoldering kettle. Maybe Gordon trusted Cole, maybe he didn't, but it was now too late to question his decision to work for him—he was committed.

Gordon came from a blue-collar family and had lived a disorderly life since he was young. He had been a roughneck for many years, but as he got older he could no longer keep up with the physical demands of the work. The job at the sugar mill paid less, but didn't require such strenuous labor, so he gladly switched careers when the opportunity arose. However, Gordon was approaching the age that most people retire and not only didn't he have any savings, he owed the bank tens of thousands from a failed oil patent he had speculated on years ago. Cole's offer was his only way out.

***

Burl's office in the Worland sheriff's department might have been a storage closet back when the building had been the county Game and Fish department. He spent very little time there, preferring to use his truck as his office when he could. His pilot helmet from Vietnam hung on the wall with a few newspaper clippings, and his desk was clear except for a small collection of files and a framed photo of his deceased wife.

"Detective Walden, thanks for speaking with me today. Hope the weather down there in Denver is as nice as it is up here," said Burl into his desk phone.

"No problem, Deputy Hutchinson, what can I do for you today?" the detective replied.

"Kind of a long shot, to be honest, but has your crew ever run into a bike gang known as Satan's Fingers?" Burl laughed a bit, as he thought it was a childish name for a group of grown men.

"Oh sure, the Fingers. We know 'em well enough. Assault,

illegal weapons, drugs, you name it. Seem to be based here in Denver, surprised they're out your way. You got something on them?"

"Nothing yet. We have us an unsolved homicide up here, and I got a report of a strange truck seen around town a few times this summer. Had a Satan's Fingers sticker on it, which the internet tells me might be a biker gang in your parts. Not much of a lead, but I don't have anything better. I'm sure you've never been there before, right?" chuckled Burl.

"Afraid I have, Deputy. If you got a tag number I can run it and see if anything comes up."

"Wish I did. All I got to go on is a late model Dodge with lots of chrome."

"Hmmm. Well, I'll make a note, but pretty slim odds anything turns up based on that description. I'll let you know, let me do some digging."

"Thanks, I appreciate it. Have a good day now." Burl stood up and paced the room. He thought he was a good deputy—traffic violations, stolen cars, occasional domestic disputes were all things he handled regularly and with confidence, but operating as a detective made him feel inept. *Should have been a brand inspector*, he thought. *Or a game warden*. Burl sat back down, lost in thought as he imagined life as a Game and Fish officer and smiling for the first time that morning.

***

The television above the bar emitted a screeching whine every time the stock cars zoomed by the camera, and it was starting to aggravate Sunny as she wiped down the bar for the night. The bar was empty except for Monty, who was watching the race and sipping the remnants of a beer.

"Monty, would you mind if I turned down the volume a bit? It's giving me a headache."

Monty looked away from the TV, nodding at Sunny. "Of course. Anything." He sat up a bit straighter in his chair and placed his arms on the bar. Sunny took the remote from the side of the cash register and pointed it at the TV. She was wearing sweatpants instead of her normal embroidered jeans.

Monty watched her work, rubbing his neatly trimmed beard. "Are you stressed? I mean, do you think the headache is from stress?"

Her back was facing him as she spoke. "I don't know.

Maybe." She wrung the rag out into the sink. "Nothing a shot of bourbon won't fix."

"Maybe a shoulder massage would help. You had a busy night here it looks." Monty cocked his head slightly sideways as he spoke.

Sunny tossed her bar rag into the sink and sighed. "It's time to go home. I'm exhausted." She walked to the register and pushed the empty drawer closed, then stared at Monty, willing him out of the bar with her eyes.

"What about that shot of bourbon? I'll have one with you." He moved closer to the edge of his stool and leaned over the bartop.

Sunny put her hands on her hips and let out a deep breath. She shook her head. "I can't do this, Monty. You should go home."

Monty tugged on his baseball cap's brim in frustration. "Can't do *what*, Sunny? I am just trying to help you."

She stared at him in silence as he stood up off his stool and buttoned up his wool vest. He picked up his beer can from the bar and threw it in the trash bin, walking briskly toward the door.

"Monty, wait..." Sunny's voice trailed off. He stopped but didn't turn around. "It's just that..." She sighed again. "After Lyle..." Sunny started crying, but with such intensity that she made no sound. Monty opened the door and walked out.

Chapter Sixteen

I think we better throw the drugs out," Pete said, his eyes not leaving the road. They had freed themselves from the traffic of Seattle two hours ago with only a short distance remaining to the Canadian border. "It's past time, in fact. I'm nervous."

Jeb was stunned. "Now? We've come all this way, and now you want to throw them out? I don't understand. These are our dreams we are sitting on. This could be everything we've ever wanted. No way." Jeb's face was getting red. "If you don't like the plan, I'll drop you off and continue the mission myself. Maybe you can hitch up to Squamish, or back to Ten Sleep, or wherever you want. I'm not giving up on this. Fuck, Pete. I thought we were in this together." Jeb's statement tapered to silence as he turned his head to stare out the passenger window.

Pete sat silently, barely containing his laughter. "I was talking about the weed, Jeb," he eventually giggled, "Let's throw the *weed* out before the border."

Jeb's face was blank as he processed Pete's statement. "Oh," Jeb said, blinking rapidly. "Yeah, better throw that out."

Pete was surprised by Jeb's emotion. "You were pissed," he taunted.

"No, I wasn't. Just sticking to the plan we had."

"Sorry, Jeb. I didn't know that money was so important to you."

"Fuck off, Stinky. You were fucking with me. Who calls weed *drugs* anyway? Not funny."

"No, I wasn't. Weed *is* a drug. If you don't believe me, ask the guards at the border up ahead." Pete turned toward Jeb, his face more serious. "We're in this together. Partners." He extended a fist toward Jeb, who bumped it with his own. Both then threw their fingers open, pretending their hands were exploding.

***

The line of cars between Pete and Jeb and the border station was almost a half-mile long, and at times it didn't seem to be moving at all. The sun was bright and with very little sea breeze blowing in from the Boundary Bay, it was hot. The pair had been quiet since entering the queue, their nervousness causing their minds to run too quickly for conversation. Jeb looked down at the van's dash and swore under his breath.

"We need to turn the heat on."

Pete looked at Jeb with astonishment. "What? The fuck we do, I'm already sweating like crazy."

Jeb shook his head. "The engine is overheating. No air moving over the radiator. The only way to cool it back down is to use the heater." Jeb reached to the heat dial of the van and cranked it over until it stopped. The heat was immediate and the already tense mood of the pair became worse. More silence ensued. Jeb thought about the temporary fix he made to the radiator back in Thermopolis, wondering if this much heat would aggravative the already delicate situation.

"It's not too late, Jeb. We don't have to go through with this," Pete finally said. "We can turn around and find another way."

Jeb rocked his head slowly. "Nope. We're here, we've committed. I found a better hiding spot for the package, wedged above the gas tank where the fuel line exits. I added another layer of garbage bag around it just in case something up there leaks. It's perfect, they will never find it. Less than an hour and we will be through—then a new era begins for us my friend." He forced a smile, clearly not as confident as he tried to sound.

"OK. You're gonna do all the talking, right?" Pete asked. "You're a better liar than I am." Jeb raised an eyebrow in response. "You know what I mean. I'm gonna crawl in the back and make a sandwich. Want one?"

"Nah, I'm good. Good luck finding anything back there, the cupboards are a bit bare."

"Hey Pete, you still napping back there?" Jeb yelled over his shoulder to the back of the van, "We're almost there, you better come back up front."

"Wasn't sleeping. Just too hot to keep my eyes open." Pete crawled over a pile of backpacks to the passenger seat. "Feeling a little funny though, hope I'm not coming down with anything."

"Probably dehydrated. Drink some water." Jeb reached down to the floorboard and grabbed a water bottle, throwing it on Pete's lap. "Find anything to eat back there? I'm starting to get a bit hungry myself."

"Nah, we ain't got shit. Had a stale oatmeal cookie that was crammed in the back of the drawer, but that's all I found. Sorry." Pete unscrewed the lid on the water bottle and took a long drink.

"Oatmeal cookie? Raisins or no raisins?"

"No raisins. It was dried out, tasted nasty."

"Shit, I've been looking for that cookie for weeks. Five grams of shrooms baked into that baby." Jeb looked over at Pete, his eyes widening. "Make like a ninja, Skinny, cause you're gettin' high-ya!"

The van pulled to a stop at the checkpoint station, heat pouring out of the open windows. Jeb handed the pair's passports to the border guard, who looked nothing like the wholesome Canadian Mountie that Jeb was expecting—his face was thick with stubble, eyes bloodshot, and tangles of greasy hair were sticking out from under his broad-brimmed hat.

"Good afternoon," the guard said dryly, eyeing the beads of sweat rolling down Jeb's face. "You feeling alright?"

Jeb wiped the sweat from his forehead. "You wouldn't believe it. Our engine started overheating back there, no air moving through the radiator and all. We had to turn the heat on to keep her cool."

The guard nodded. "Happens all the time when the line is backed up in the summer. Most don't know the heater trick though." He hacked into his fist, then cleared his throat rather explosively.

"What about you, do you feel alright?" Jeb asked. "That cough sounds nasty."

The guard scowled back at Jeb, his left eye twitching spastically, then turned his gaze towards their passports. He typed slowly at his keyboard, hidden out of view. Pete sat perfectly still, staring straight ahead through the windshield, occasionally darting an eye to the guard but never turning his head. His body was beginning to vibrate.

"What brings you to Canada?"

"Climbing, sir."

"Climbers, eh? I'll mark your occupations as vagrants then?"

Jeb glanced at Pete, confused. "We are both unemployed at the moment."

"Where are you staying?"

"In our van, sir. In the parking lot for the Chief."

"Is that legal?" The guard looked over his glasses at Jeb.

"As far as we know. Never been hassled before." Jeb pointed a thumb toward Pete. "Loverboy here might be staying with his girlfriend." Jeb laughed, but Pete didn't move from his nearly frozen position.

"Girlfriend? Got a picture?" The guard pushed his glasses back up his nose, peering over Jeb at Pete, his eye still twitching.

Pete finally looked at the guard, confused. He lowered his eyebrows and squinted, trying to make sense of the question. "No. Why would you need that?" Pete's speech was slow and labored.

The guard looked back down at his keyboard and shook his head. "Never mind. How much money do you have with you?"

"Never enough, am-I-right?" Jeb joked but the guard's expression remained serious. Jeb's smile disappeared. "Less than ten thousand dollars, if that is what you are asking. Waaay less."

"Any handguns, shotguns, rifles, explosives, or fireworks?"

"No, sir."

"Brass knuckles?"

"What?"

"Never mind. Do you have any beer or liquor?"

"Yes, sir. We have some beer in the cooler."

"How much?"

"Less than half a rack," Jeb said, proud that he remembered the legal limit for transporting beer into Canada from his previous trips.

"Alright. How about cigarettes?"

"Half a pack of rolling tobacco, sir."

The guard typed a few more notes silently. In the passenger seat, Pete was deep in the mushroom cookie haze. His eyes felt like they were bulging out of his face, dry and burning. The mild fear he had felt minutes ago was quickly becoming paranoia. He could feel the guard staring at him, almost like he could see through him completely, down to the secrets he was trying to hide. *Best to not look at him,* Pete thought. He was grinding his teeth, his jaw moving noticeably.

The guard finally looked up from his typing, glancing over at Pete. "What's going on with you over there? You don't look so well." Pete's eyes shifted slightly to the guard as he tried to smile.

"I'm just hot, sir. I might not be..."

Jeb interrupted him quickly. "If you ask me, I think he is a bit nervous about seeing his girlfriend."

The guard sighed. "Must be quite the lady for you to be that pale and sweaty. Wish you had a picture." He turned his attention back to Jeb. "Looks like you have been to Mexico recently. What were you doing down there?"

"Climbing, sir. Potrero Chico, a few winters ago," Jeb replied.

"Score any *mota* down there?"

"No, sir. Don't touch the stuff."

"Uh-huh." The guard seemed disinterested in his answer. "Did you go to Acapulco?"

Jeb frowned, confused. "Uh, no. Just Potrero. I think Acapulco is a long way away from Potrero, isn't it?"

The guard looked at Jeb, seeing his confusion. "Just wondering, I've heard Acapulco is nice. Do you have any fruits or vegetables?"

"I don't think we have food of any kind, sir. Pete here ate the last cookie." Jeb looked over at Pete and laughed, but Pete's mind was flush with too many other thoughts to react.

"No food? That makes it easy. Do you have any pepper spray? If it's for bears it's allowed, but not if it's for people."

Jeb squinted, trying to understand. "That's weird. But no pepper spray. Of any kind."

"Any bug spray?"

"No."

"Get some once you cross, you'll need it. Bugs are bad this time of year." For the first time, the guard seemed to smile.

Jeb looked relieved. He sat back deep in his chair, suddenly looking much more relaxed.

"But first, we gotta search your vehicle."

***

Jeb sat on the curb, his back to the sun, picking up gravel and throwing it at a water drainage grate in front of him. Pete was lying on his back on the sidewalk, knees up and arms flailed out to the side, his baseball cap shading his face from the sun. The van was a short distance in front of them, its former contents now encircling it. Even the passenger seat had been removed and was currently sitting on the blacktop. One agent dug through the plastic storage bins that had been excavated from the van, another laid on his back below it, searching the undercarriage with his flashlight.

Pete muttered something, mostly incoherent. Jeb wasn't sure he understood it but guessed at the meaning by context. Pete rolled over on his side, away from where Jeb was seated. Jeb picked up another pebble and threw it at the grate. He watched an officer crouch by a tire and lean his face near the valve. He pressed into the valve, sniffing the escaping puff of air. The other officer loaded a bit into a cordless drill, ducking under the van before drilling a hole somewhere underneath.

"Fuck," Jeb muttered under his breath, "pretty fucking thorough." His steady optimism cracked and desperation washed over him, his head hanging low. He thought back to a childhood summer when he and his mother had driven all through the south, hiding from Jeb's abusive father. He had understood his mother's panic clearly and knew that he needed to help. Fearlessness and frivolity were already a part of Jeb's personality, but now he saw they helped his mother be brave and unworried herself—traits that he maintained from that point onward. Jeb committed to staying strong for Pete if not for himself.

"This is why we wrote the note. We aren't stuffed yet, gotta stay positive." Jeb said, feigning confidence. As he finished speaking, he saw a piece of paper fly from the pile of gear on the ground, picked up by the swirling wind. Could it be their note? His hope sunk further as he resisted the urge to chase after it, knowing that if it was, it was too late.

One agent walked over to the other as he crawled out from under the van, squatting down next to him. The pair engaged in discussion for a while before both stood up. One walked back over to the office headquarters, removing his latex gloves in the process, while the other walked straight toward Pete and Jeb. He was wearing a protective vest over his uniform, clearly armed with both a handgun and a taser. He carried a black plastic garbage bag, cradled like an infant.

Jeb reached out and patted Pete on the knee. Pete sat up,

rubbing his eyes. "Be tough Pete. We will get through this." Jeb was speaking uncharacteristically fast, and the volume of his voice increasing. His body was tense. "Do lots of pull-ups in prison and we can leave stronger than when we go in." He took a deep breath, then exhaled loudly. "Love ya, buddy."

The agent stopped in front of the pair, a scowl on his face. He took off his sunglasses with his free hand, hanging them from a strap on his flak jacket. "Stand up. You two are coming with me," he said as he gestured down the sidewalk leading to the building ahead.

He led them to a small dark room inside the hallway, shutting the door behind him as he stepped back out. Jeb and Pete heard the door lock.

"I'm sorry, Pete. This is my fault." Jeb scanned Pete, trying to understand his mental state, seeing that his eyes were welling with tears. "I shouldn't have been so greedy. We had everything we needed. Now we got nothing."

Pete finally spoke, his voice surprisingly clear. "It's not your fault—I agreed to all this. I had nothing before except an unfinished thesis and a chance with Lydia. Nothing really. We rolled the dice and lost."

The door opened and an officer they hadn't yet seen stepped in, carrying the black plastic bag. He was a wearing a blue blazer, not the uniforms the other officers wore, making Jeb believe he was of higher rank. He threw the bag onto the table in front of them with a loud thud.

"You didn't think we would find this, did ya?"

Jeb stared at the black plastic bag. His heartbeat was redlining. He closed his eyes slowly, reaching deep to find enough composure to speak. "Find what, sir?"

The agent grabbed the edge of the bag with his gloved hand, pulling it back to reveal the bag's contents. "Do you know how stupid it is to try to smuggle this into Canada?"

Jeb and Pete sat stunned, unable to lift their gazes from the package's contents.

Jeb spoke first, his face pale. "Firewood?"

The agent violently pushed the bag and the two pieces of split pine off the table and onto the floor. "Yes, firewood! A single piece could destroy our forests, ruin our economy. This log could be crawling with budworms, loopers, and pine beetles, and that's just the insects. Rusts, molds, fungi, what have you. Reckless, the two of you. It's a ten-billion-dollar industry, ya know." He paused, low on breath. "The pride of His Majesty's Government, our forests are."

Jeb and Pete were both staring at the guard, their expressions matched in their amazement. "Sorry, sir," said Jeb, "I didn't know we couldn't bring in firewood. Won't happen again." The agent picked the bag off the ground, wrapping the edges of the bag back over the firewood. He wiped a bit of spit from the edge of his lip with the back of his glove.

"Better not—we've got notes on you now. Pack up your vehicle and get out of here. We'll dispose of….this." He opened the door and left the room, shaking his head and muttering under his breath as he walked. For the first time in at least an hour, Pete's face had a noticeable expression—one of surprise and amazement.

"I told you it would work," Jeb said, standing from his chair. He reached out and pulled Pete to his feet. "Ye of little faith."

CHAPTER SEVENTEEN

"Danimal!" yelled Jeb from across the empty parking lot in Vancouver's east side, pumping his fist with enthusiasm. Even at a distance, Dan looked different—thin, hollow, and moving less fluidly than Jeb had remembered. He held his arms out and ran towards Dan, the two embracing as they met.

"It's been too long," Dan said as he pounded his fist into Jeb's back.

"You look trim, my friend. You on a sport climber's diet? But that beard makes up for it—you look like a proper fucking lumberjack!" Jeb joked. "I thought you got paid to plant trees, not cut them down."

Dan ignored the comment, turning to Pete. "Pete, how are ya?"

"Doing great, Dan. Thanks for, uh, accommodating us," said Pete, widening his eyes to indicate the double meaning. Pete was still a bit high from the cookie.

"No problem. We'll talk business later. Let's get a beer and catch up." Dan patted them both on the back as they walked toward the bar.

The Boyle Bar on East Hastings street was originally targeted to be an upscale British pub serving the more affluent residents of Vancouver. The students of nearby Simon Fraser University, however, found the old-world charm irresistibly clichéd, and rapidly displaced the intended audience. The slow decline from upscale pub to college dive bar was well underway, but perhaps yet from complete. The trio sat at the empty bar underneath a dusty banner, bottles of beer in front of them. Jeb and Pete recalled the night they found the wreckage and drugs, their plan for smuggling it across the border, and their close call with the search.

"That's quite the story," said Dan after. His eyes were baggy and shades darker than the rest of his face. "You boys have no idea how lucky you were to find that package, not to mention getting it across the border the way you did. Why didn't you tell me about that part of the plan? I could have arranged something much safer—you're lucky you got through."

"No way," said Jeb, "that plan was bomber. It worked, didn't it?"

Dan looked at Jeb sideways. "Be careful confusing luck with success. Any idea who the dead guy was? Somebody is probably looking for that package, right?"

"No idea who the dude was, but you are right—in hindsight we should have split town a little quicker. Pete and I still had some unfinished climbing projects though. Still do, actually." Jeb took a swig of beer. "I can't believe you don't like our double blind mule scheme. It was solid."

Dan shook his head. "Fuckin' A. You've always loved rolling the dice. How long are you guys going to be in Squamish? I need a week or so to arrange a deal with my connections."

"Well, that depends on old Pete here—Lydia is there, so my guess is that he will want to stay until the rainy season starts. Isn't that right, Pete?"

"We'll see. I don't even know if she's still into me. She seemed a little dodgy when I talked to her last week. Speaking of which, I better call and tell her when we'll get there. Jeb, you think we'll be up there by noon tomorrow?"

"Hopefully by noon. We'll have to wait and see what kind of hangover Dan can give us tonight." Jeb laughed, patting Dan on the back. Pete stood up and fished his phone from his pocket, then walked outside to call Lydia.

"Good to see you man," said Jeb after Pete had left. "It's been too long."

"You too." Dan paused, his voice suddenly more urgent when he started speaking again. "Jeb, I need some help."

"Anything for you Danimal!" said Jeb, not recognizing Dan's change in tone.

"No, it's serious. I'm using again. Been trying to quit, it never seems to take." Dan was fidgeting with his coaster, trying to avoid making eye contact with Jeb.

"Ah, fuck man. I thought you kicked that shit."

"I did for a while. It's worse this time. Not gonna lie, I need help."

"OK. Of course. What can I do?"

"Don't know. You can't be around me here, not right now—I'm in a bit of trouble with some people in town."

"Fuck. What kind of trouble?"

"I owe some people some money. I'm planning on paying them back with my cut of the money we make. Should be good after that. Just don't want you near me until then."

"Heavy." Jeb exhaled loudly while he thought. "Want to come up to Squamish for a bit. Maybe a change of scenery would be good. We'll help you, however we can."

"Yeah, that might be good." Dan looked unsure. "Let me get your money and we'll go from there."

Jeb sat in silence, suddenly questioning the plan to involve Dan. The weight loss, the dark eyes, the fidgeting—Dan was clearly an addict, but now his veiled suggestion of violence and his plan to buy them off with the heroin made Jeb regret the path they had committed to.

"Could I climb with you in Squamish?" Dan said. "Once I clean up and kick the jonsin', I mean."

"Of course you can!" Jeb slapped Dan on the back of his shoulder, hiding his apprehension. "It would be great to share a rope with you again, brother."

"I think you're right, getting out of here will help me quit. And I need some friends around. I hope I can still climb—I miss it."

"It would be good to have you back. We've had some adventures together, huh?"

"Sure have. And hopefully will again."

"Climber's bond, right? Something happens during those sleepless bivouacs, near disasters, bluebird summit days. I'd do anything for my partners."

"Me too." Dan put an arm around Jeb and pulled him in for a hug, ignoring the stares of the other patrons in the bar.

***

As Jeb and Pete rounded the corner of Howe Sound into the Squamish River valley, the imposing profile of the Grand Wall came into view—the longest, most vertical aspect of the granite monolith called the Stawamus Chief. The Chief, known as *Siám' Smánit* to the indigenous Squamish people, is a spiritual place for many, the native tribe and climbers included. Climbers and geologists, on first sight of the Chief, immediately notice the intruding black dike of dolerite rock that slices the entire face vertically. The Squamish legend says that this feature was created by a fearsome two-headed sea serpent as it climbed the face pursued by a young warrior determined to slay it. Geologists theorize that it was magma flowing into a crack in the plutonic dome. Jeb and Pete were once lured into climbing the dike by its striking aesthetic, only to be disappointed to find the rock quality of the dolerite was not nearly as good as the surrounding granite. Geologists and storytellers, however, are not let down by the dike in any such way.

For Jeb, the sight of the Chief triggered a complex feeling of homecoming, both peaceful and comforting, mixed with some nostalgia and a tiny bit of dread. Jeb felt at home among the mossy forests below the walls, as well as on the textured white granite itself. He knew that he would be back with his people— the irreverent but inspired tribe of climbers. It was as close to a home as he felt about anywhere, outside of the van and Ten Sleep, and these were his friends and fellow tribesmen. The dread, small enough that Jeb might not have noticed it for more than an instant, was due to the overwhelming scale of the formation. Even though he had seen it, stood underneath it, and climbed it many times, he felt the presence of the monolith *emotionally*.

Pete was too preoccupied about his upcoming reunion with Lydia to do more than glance at the Chief. Their last time together ended with Pete asking Lydia to chase good weather with him for the winter, but she declined, stating jobs, visas, and other excuses that Pete didn't believe. He suspected that Lydia might want someone more rooted and stable, someone with a career path or at least a little more money. When he called to tell her of his trip to Squamish, however, she seemed genuinely excited to see him, putting Pete in a similar emotional state as Jeb—exhilaration mixed with a little dread.

"Hey Jeb," said Pete. "Do you think I should grow a beard like Dan? Lydia might like beards, living up here with the lumberjacks and woodsman and all."

Jeb laughed before he realized Pete was serious. "No, you shouldn't grow a beard. Your boyish good looks make up for some serious personality disorders you know." Pete wasn't smiling. "Just kidding. Lydia has you all tangled up, huh?"

"Fuck off, Jeb. You don't understand. I am just saying that if I don't mind having a beard and Lydia likes beards, why wouldn't I grow one?"

"And that is very sweet of you, Pete," laughed Jeb. "I am just saying that you should be plain old Skinny Pete and Lydia will love you like the rest of us do. Plus, from the looks of that scraggle already on your face, I doubt you could grow a proper beard anyway. I'm rooting for you here, man—believe me. I would love to have the van to myself for a while—stretch out, snore, not listen to your shit music."

"My music isn't shit." Pete looked slightly insulted. "OK. Then help me out: Don't tell Lydia about the drugs, she wouldn't approve. Second, can you lend me a couple hundred bucks 'til we get our money? I'm pretty low on cash and I don't want to look like a total dirtbag. I'd love to take Lydia out to dinner."

"Look like a dirtbag? Some things you can't hide, beard or no beard." He and Pete laughed together as they pulled into the parking lot below the Stawamus Chief.

"I'll give you a hundo when we get settled. Once Dan shows up I probably won't even care if you pay me back," Jeb said as he rolled the van to a stop and shut off the engine.

"Do you think it's a good idea to have Dan up here? He seems different than before. Something's off."

"It will be alright, Stinky. He needs us right now. I'll fill you in later." Jeb nodded to Pete, trying to assure him. "Plus, he's bringing us a fuck-ton of money."

Chapter Eighteen

Dan knew the Triads wanted to kill him but he didn't fully understand why. The disagreement started after police confiscated a brick of heroin during a bust of a street-level dealer who had been working under Dan. The Triad looked to Dan for compensation, who argued the loss was part of business and should be absorbed by the top. A minor recompense would have satisfied the lost honor—even a simple acknowledgement of his misdeed might have worked—but Dan had denied them either. He didn't understand the complexities of face and honor used by the Hóng Lóng, and perhaps in the depths of his addiction he ignored the danger they represented— or just didn't care. His newfound clarity made him regret his prior ignorance and made him fear for his life, a feeling he hadn't missed in the years spent numb from heroin.

His plan was to use the package from Jeb and Pete to buy himself out of trouble. He would sell the heroin to the Triad at half its normal wholesale cost and forfeit his cut. Pete and Jeb would still make more money than they had ever seen, and he would make peace with the Triad.

Dan took his time climbing up the rusted metal stairs on the back of the port-side warehouse, prepping his sales pitch to Chen one last time. He knocked on the steel door twice before opening it. Chen's escort Hulin walked briskly to the door, reaching for the handgun tucked in his belt before Chen called him off.

"He's OK, Hulin," said Chen as he sneered at Dan. "He says he has an offer too good to refuse." Chen's sneer transformed into a feigned smile as he turned his attention to Dan. "Good afternoon, Dan. You are quite brave to show back up here." Chen folded his hands and leaned back in his chair. "As you may know, I have orders from the Mountain Master to kill you."

Dan had suspected their intent, of course, but hearing the confirmation of his death sentence caused his stomach to knot even tighter.

"Yes, sir. I apologize for the misunderstanding; I want to make it right. My offer will compensate you ten-fold." He glanced over his shoulder at the man posted at the door, trying to determine if there was any chance to get by him before he or Chen could draw their guns and fire. Dan placed his messenger bag on the table in front of Chen and motioned to him to open it. Chen took out the package, still wrapped in layers of brown paper and cellophane from Jeb and Pete's undercarriage smuggling efforts. He looked at Dan, awaiting an explanation.

Dan took the cue. "Three *keys*—as pure as it gets. It's yours for two hundred, as we agreed. Parcel it out and you'll triple that on the street. Cut it down, you'll quadruple it." He looked at Chen nervously.

"And where did you happen upon this gift?"

"I stole it from the Brother's Keepers," said Dan, referencing a rival Vancouver gang. "I killed one of them to get it for you. I wanted to make everything right."

Chen tapped his fingers on the table. "Very interesting. Why do you suppose I haven't heard about the death of a Brother?"

"Maybe he was too small a player. Maybe they are embarrassed that I pulled it off. I don't know."

Chen stared at Dan, studying his face. He opened the top drawer of his desk and took out a small knife. He cut a small slit in the middle of the package with the pen knife and pulled out one of the packets. He nodded to Hulin, who took the packet and disappeared in the hallway behind Chen.

"If the product is pure, your offer is indeed generous. It should repay your debt to me," said Chen. He smiled softly at Dan, who let out a small breath as some of the tension left his chest. "The Mountain Master may require a separate gift as well, as you have greatly damaged his honor. I will talk to him and try to ease his frustrations." Chen rapped his fingers on the desk. "Perhaps he will listen."

Tension rushed back into Dan's body. "Thanks," Dan said, staring down at the floor as he pondered what else might be required to clear his debt. He looked up at Chen, who was still staring at Dan intently. The two shared the uncomfortable silence as Hulin walked back into the room.

"It's pure, boss. Very pure," said Hulin, handing Chen a vial filled with orange liquid. Chen admired it briefly, before handing it back to Hulin.

"Very good. Dan, it looks like you get to live a little longer. You've done well." Chen opened the bottom drawer of his desk and retrieved five stacks of bills, placing them in front of Dan. "You're free to go."

Dan put the cash in his messenger bag, which went over his shoulder. He bowed slightly to Chen, as it seemed appropriate although he wasn't really sure.

"Thank you, Chen," Dan said, bowing again as he backed out the door.

Chapter Nineteen

Pete and Lydia were sitting side-by-side at the top of the sixth pitch of The Grand Wall. The ledge was flat and spacious, providing a comfortable spot for them to sit as Pete belayed Jeb on the pitch above. Lydia rested her head onto Pete's shoulder—her helmet was hard on his bony frame, but he didn't care. He was climbing perfect granite, high above the valley floor, the weather was perfect, and Lydia was cuddling up next to him. Pete could have stayed on the ledge for hours.

"So good!" called Jeb from above. He had just transitioned from the juggy face into the thin corner crack, which was just wide enough for his fingers to fit in. His left foot was smashed into the corner, his right smearing on a slight depression of the face as he shook out his left arm, trying to give it a bit of rest. "So good," he said again, this time to himself. Pete hadn't been paying much attention to Jeb, only paying out rope to him as he felt him need it. It wasn't a textbook belay, but rather more of a telepathic one that happens after a long time of climbing with someone.

"I've missed you since Joshua Tree," Lydia said. "That was a great trip, eh?"

Pete smiled. Lydia telling him that she missed him was about as affectionate as she got, and it felt great. "Yeah, what a trip. We should meet up there again this winter."

"You know, I've been thinking about that lately. I think it might be time to-"

Jeb fell without warning, pulling Pete up off the ledge by the rope that connected the two.

"What the fuck, Jeb?" yelled Pete. "What happened?"

"Whoo hoo!" yelled Jeb loudly. "Sorry about that. Foot slipped." He started climbing again as Pete retook his seat next to Lydia.

"What a kook. Slipped off right before the top." Pete laughed as he started paying out rope again. After a few moments of silence, he looked at Lydia seriously. "Now, what were you saying before?"

"Well, I was just thinking about the miles between us last winter, and with how busy the Coffee Crush has been lately, and I'm just not sure-"

"Off belay!" interrupted Jeb again. He began to pull in the slack of the ropes.

Pete freed the rope from his belay device and yelled up: "You're off!" He turned his attention to Lydia, his heart in his throat. "You're not sure of what?"

Lydia paused, looking as seriously as Pete had seen her. "Well, I think it might be-"

"On belay!" yelled Jeb again from above. "Climb on red rope!"

"Let's talk about it later," Lydia said, leaning close and trying to kiss Pete on the cheek before their helmets collided. "Oops," laughed Lydia. "Climbing on red rope!" she yelled back at Jeb. Lydia stepped off the tower and started up, leaving Pete alone with his thoughts on the pedestal.

"Not sure of what?" he muttered to himself. His head was spinning with possibilities when his rope went taut.

"Climb on blue rope!" Jeb yelled, and Pete started up behind Lydia. His movement was not his usual smooth, flowing motion, and his footwork was imprecise. His head was too cloudy, too crowded, to climb well. He needed a clear mind to be able to enter the black hole of focused movement, and he didn't have it. One thought was difficult for him to repress. *Why am I always the one chasing?*

Chapter Twenty

Chen was sitting at his desk pondering his good fortune. Dan's offer was almost a gift and one that would pay off handsomely. Chen had not informed the Mountain Master of this development and did not intend to. He could convince the Master to commute the death sentence of Dan and keep the unexpected profit himself. Or, he thought, he could kill Dan anyway and cover his tracks. One final payoff before packing his new motorhome and escaping the life of a gangster forever. He closed his eyes, imagining the roaring falls of the rugged Oregon coast and the deep red sandstone canyons of the desert Southwest. His childhood self would never have believed that he would escape the rooftop slums of Kowloon and be touring the storybook American West in a luxury van.

"Master Chen!" shouted Hulin, rushing down the hallway waving a piece of paper. "I found this letter inside of the package." He handed it to Chen.

Dear law enforcement of the great country of Canada,

We apologize for what is probably a confusing situation. If you are reading this, you have found the drugs. They were intended for a cartel in Vancouver, but thanks to your diligent policing they will not reach their destination now. We admire your effort—you are a worthy adversary, whether or not we agree with your mission.

Neither the drugs nor this letter are the property of whoever they were found with. Most likely, this package was found on the underside of a truck or van, cellophane protecting it from the weather. It was to be collected by the Canadian cartel once the vehicle crossed the border, the description of the vehicle and its drivers being relayed by us (the source) to them (the purchasers). The driver(s) of the vehicle have absolutely no knowledge of this process or package and are not to be blamed.

If you would like further proof, I recommend you contact the purchasers, as we are sure you are already quite aware of their operation and their names. They are the most dangerous group in Vancouver, after all. They will confirm this story.

As for us, we are very peaceful drug importers who do not want to endanger our unsuspecting transporters. They are simply the victims of your pointless war on drugs. Please let them go.

Sincerely,
Drug Dealers

Chen's entire body tightened with anger. *That lying laowei motherfucker!* He clenched his fists and pounded them into the table, his mouth pursing tightly. "I will kill Dan myself!"

Chapter Twenty-One

Cole had been introduced to Pigeon, the captain of the Denver chapter of the Satan's Fingers outlaw motorcycle gang, through a fellow Marine veteran he had served with in Afghanistan. The Fingers were looking for a supplier and Cole was seeking a customer, so a loose and sometimes tenuous partnership was formed. The Fingers were a small group, primarily involved in drugs and counterfeit cash in the Rocky Mountain West, but actively recruiting and expanding operations wherever they could.

Cole was convinced that the Fingers were responsible for Lyle's murder and his missing drugs—there weren't other explanations. He dreaded the idea of accusing Pigeon as it would threaten their business arrangement, but the longer he sat on the thought of the Fingers crossing him, the hotter his anger grew. He picked up his mobile phone and dialed.

"Pigeon, it's Big Bear," Cole said into the phone. He understood the ridiculousness of his *nom de guerre*, but during the first meeting with Pigeon a year ago, he had panicked and said the first name he could think of. Years of service in foreign wars gave Cole an education he didn't get growing up in Wyoming, but he was still very naive about operating in black-markets.

"Of course it's you, *Big Bear*," Pigeon laughed, "I've got your number in my phone. What year do you think this is?"

Cole didn't share Pigeon's amusement. "You killed my driver; you stole my packages. I need answers—they better be good ones."

"Easy man. I've got no idea what you are talking about.

That's not how we do business. I think you're after the wrong people, my friend," said Pigeon with a calm tone. "We didn't kill anyone, and we don't have your *H*."

"I don't believe you. I need my packages or I need my payment—your choice. You have two more days to decide."

Cole hung up and threw his phone against the wall.

***

"Morning, Paul. Thanks for letting me stop by." Burl walked into the coroner's office and shut the door behind him. "I've got a bunch of leads, but none of them seem to be heading anywhere. It's been almost a month and all I have to show is a bunch of dead ends. Thought I'd bounce a few things off you if you don't mind."

"No problem, Burl." Paul pushed a couple of folders off to the side of his desk and motioned to the chair in front. "Have a seat."

"Thanks," said Burl. "Did you find anything else about that bullet? I went back out to the scene. Didn't find any more shells outside of that .22. Of course, if you look at any patch of dirt in Wyoming hard enough you'll find one of them."

"Afraid all I can tell you about that bullet is that it was a .38. The crime lab just can't tell much more than that. Of course, if we had a gun they could tell you if it was the one that fired it."

"Figured that." Burl frowned, staring at the floor. "Is there anything you found that would make you think that he was killed somewhere else and then put in his truck before it was forced off the road? That might explain a few things."

"I don't think so, Burl. His head injury was consistent with going through the windshield. Pretty sure it was what killed him, as I said before. Outside of a few other lacerations, likely from the glass as well, the only other obvious injury was the broken ribs. And I figure you broke those when you were trying to resuscitate him," Paul said. "You don't have to push that hard, you know. Just enough to compress the chest by an inch or two."

"Resuscitate him? I never tried. Body was already cold by the time I got there. Why do you think I tried CPR?"

Paul shrugged his shoulders. "If it wasn't you, it was someone else. Along with the broken ribs, there were clear handprints on his shirt near his chest, in blood. I thought it had to be you." Paul rubbed his chin while he thought. "Couldn't have been the murderer, right? Why would you shoot someone and then try to bring them back to life?" Paul laughed. "Then again, I'm no detective!"

"I'm afraid I'm not either. Somebody else must have gotten to the scene before I did." Burl paused and pondered the scenario. "We never did find out who called it in, maybe it was that feller. He sure sounded nervous on the 911 tape, wouldn't give us any details." Burl sighed. "Maybe he stole that damn horse and didn't want us to find out. It was worth a lot of money, you know."

"Are you still hung up on that horse? You seem as concerned about that horse as with who killed Lyle."

"I know it might look that way, but the horse is the only motive I have so far. You find the horse, you find the killer. That's what I think anyway." Burl rose up out of his chair. "Thanks for your time today, Paul. I got some work to do."

***

Sunny sat in the living room of the small single-story house she had shared with Lyle, surrounded by cardboard boxes. It had taken her a long time to find the energy to sort through the remainder of his possessions, but she couldn't put it off any longer. A clean house might help her clear her mind, and if she was truly going to leave Ten Sleep, most of the clutter would need to be discarded. Leaving was still merely an abstract idea—no plans had been made nor a destination decided, but the immediacy of the idea was growing. She had clung onto her dreams of better days for too long without acting to find them, hoping instead that they might find her. She recently realized the futility of this thought.

The clothes and books could be easily donated. The fishing tackle and hunting gear would command a fair sum at a garage sale. The boxes of photos, she thought, could be sorted later, or just thrown away. It was the arrowheads, points, and scrapers she felt conflicted about. She knew that many museums or private collectors would pay a high price, but Lyle had always told her they weren't his to sell—a principle he held onto even when money was scarce.

She picked out a small arrowhead, perfectly symmetrical, chipped from hard gray chert. She pushed the point into her open palm, imagining what it's serrations might do to flesh at speed. How many such points were left to find? How many might never be? It was a question that Lyle had proposed to her years ago, and one that she disregarded at the time. She never shared his fascination of history. Sunny always had accused Lyle of living too much in the past instead of in the moment, letting his point hunts distract him from house maintenance, finding better work, even nurturing their relationship. She knew now that she had resented him for it. Lyle's question of unfindable treasure suddenly anguished her, even if she had no guess to its answer.

Chapter Twenty-Two

Gordon parked his truck on the shoulder of the highway between the first and second switchbacks, shut off the engine, and climbed out. He didn't know exactly where Lyle's truck had gone off the road, but from the newspaper's description of the accident, he knew he could get close. As he walked through the sagebrush between the two hairpins, he found enough broken glass to confirm his hunch. Cole had assured him that he had searched the site for the boxes the day after the accident and hadn't found anything, but Gordon's trust in Cole had been deteriorating. In fact, Gordon wasn't sure that Cole hadn't killed Lyle himself.

He followed the trail of glass and snapped-off sage further down the hillside, near the creek, then walked up through the trees that lined the bank, finding nothing. He sat down on a boulder next to the creek, delaying both the hike back up the hill but also returning to town empty-handed.

Gordon heard some sounds across the creek, near the old dirt road that mirrored Highway 16 on the other side of Ten Sleep Creek. He always thought it was funny that everyone referred to it as the *old highway*, as with its washboards and potholes nobody would call it a *highway* on its own. Still, the largely abandoned road was popular with climbers and hunters for the abundance of unregulated camping, with views and convenience unrivaled by the official paid campgrounds above and below the canyon. Gordon moved to a clearing to see where the sounds were coming from, spotting a couple of climbers making their morning breakfast. He walked along the creek, his pace now quickened, looking for a spot to cross. He found a section of rocks and started across, precariously balancing on slick boulders in his even slicker cowboy boots. He cursed out loud as his arms whirled above his head trying to keep his balance. Once he reached the other side, he walked up the hill toward the campers, trying to appear as if he was on a casual stroll.

"Morning!" Gordon yelled as he approached, feigning a smile on his face.

"Hi," one of the climbers said, startled by the sudden presence of a stranger. "Howzit going?"

"Dandy. Beautiful morning for a walk, I reckon." Gordon pulled on his mustache. "Take it you boys are rock climbers. Been camped here for long?"

"Nah, we just got in last night. Long drive from Boulder. We had just enough time for a campfire and few beers before we crashed," said the man, nodding towards a handful of crushed cans lying on the ground near the fire ring. "Wished I hadn't had that last one, if you know what I mean!"

Gordon looked towards the beer cans and fire pit, spotting a partially burned box with a familiar marking. He walked over to the pit and grabbed what cardboard remained. The logo was no longer entirely legible, but Gordon knew the box was from Worland Sugar Company—the same boxes he normally packed Lyle's deliveries in. Gordon's calm evaporated.

"Did you find anything else when you got here?" His sudden change in tone surprised the other two men.

"No," one of the climbers said, confused by Gordon's interest in a burned box. "There was a pile of wood and couple of glass bottles in the fire pit. We just built a stack of logs and threw some white gas on it. Boom! Boy Scout fire!"

Gordon wasn't paying attention. He rummaged around the campsite, looking for more boxes or clues. He kicked over a pile of wood next to the fire pit, then walked to a pad of trampled grass next to the climber's parked Subaru. He paused in front of a small dark spot in the dirt, kneeling down in front of it. Gordon stuck his finger in the spot and examined the greasy dirt that stuck to it. The climber's watched in confusion as Gordon sniffed the tip of his finger with an audible whiff before sticking his finger to his tongue.

"Anti-freeze," mumbled Gordon under his breath. "Those goddamn boys in the Econoline."

CHAPTER TWENTY-THREE

Burl sat in his parked truck in an industrial district near Denver, surrounded by steel-sided warehouses and pavement, holding a bag of pistachios in his lap. He cracked a pistachio and ate the nut, then nested the two shell halves together before flicking the shells out the passenger side window. Outside, the ground was littered with shells, but even more shells were inside of the cab.

Stakeouts were a new experience for Burl, and he wasn't sure he was doing it right. Detective Walden had given him the address of the warehouse in Denver, but he hadn't seen anything unusual all morning. Perhaps he'd set up too close and scared off the gang. He'd certainly seen that happen before in detective shows, which constituted the majority of his investigative experience.

"Waste of time," Burl said to himself, flicking one last stack of shells out the window. He grabbed his keys from the dashboard and put them in the ignition. Just as he started his truck, a vehicle approached from behind and pulled in next to the curb. He watched in his rearview mirror as a man got out of the truck and entered the building. It was the first movement at the warehouse all morning.

Burl shut the engine back off. He stared intently for a few minutes before returning his attention to his pistachio game. He cracked a shell with his thumbnail as the sound of a muffled gunshot came from the building. Burl froze, not sure what to do. He had no evidence, warrant, or jurisdiction, and less-than-textbook understanding of probable cause. Worse, in his years as law enforcement he had never been involved in an armed conflict. Burl took a deep breath and opened the truck door.

He approached the entrance, unholstering his handgun. He cracked the door until he could see inside. An empty hallway ran the length of the building. He opened the door quickly and stepped inside. "Police! I'm armed!" he yelled. Burl paused and listened but heard nothing.

He approached the first door in the hallway. Holding his breath, he pulled it open and stepped in. There was nothing inside the room except a few stacks of boxes. He crept down the hallway to the next door. As he drew close, chaos erupted inside of the room—a gunshot, followed by breaking glass. Burl reached for the door's handle just as it burst open, knocking him onto his back, his head hitting the concrete with a thud. Before his vision cleared, two men fled past him.

***

Pigeon stared at Cole, unfazed by the gun pointed at him. He folded his arms to show his calm, his namesake pigeon tattoo clear on his forearm. A large knife hung from his belt. Mad Dog stood a few feet away from Pigeon, his black vest propped open by his protruding belly.

"I need the heroin or I need the cash." Cole's gun drifted to Mad Dog. Mad Dog grinned, running his fingers through his long black hair.

"Whatcha gonna do, big man? Shoot us both? Even if we had your junk that wouldn't help you much."

Cole quickly aimed his gun at the floor between them and fired a round. Pigeon and Mad Dog jumped in opposite directions, Pigeon diving behind a stack of boxes as Mad Dog rolled against the wall. Mad Dog grabbed a small pistol from his ankle holster before getting back to his feet. Cole backpedaled and returned his aim to Mad Dog.

"We don't have your H and we didn't kill your man. Why would we kill the guy that makes us money?" Pigeon said, pulling his leather vest straight.

Cole pointed his gun at Pigeon, then back at Mad Dog quickly. Pigeon nodded to Mad Dog, who started to flank Cole. Pigeon took a step closer and pulled his knife from its sheath.

It was a stalemate—Cole couldn't see any good path forward. He fired his gun near Pigeon for cover, then picked up a chair and hurled it through the window. He jumped through, tucking his head and rolling as he hit the grass outside. He ran down the alley toward his truck, looking over his shoulder for the Fingers. His sprint slowed as he neared his truck.

Cole opened the driver's door and jumped in, starting it immediately and shifting into gear. His eyes paused briefly on the truck in front of him as he pulled by—he knew the truck and its owner, the veteran plates from Washakie County confirming his suspicion. It was alarming but it would have to wait—Pigeon and Mad Dog had burst through the warehouse door and were running towards him. Cole sunk the accelerator to the floorboard and sped down the street.

CHAPTER TWENTY-FOUR

The first night of Dan's withdrawals was terrifying for Jeb to witness—he couldn't imagine what they were like for Dan. He spent most of the night writhing, muscles twitching spastically, vomiting on the floor. Jeb brought him water and towels—dry ones for the sweat and vomit, wet ones for his forehead that seemed to calm his strained breathing. Neither Dan nor Jeb slept much at all.

The second night was slightly better, although Dan still spent much of the evening shivering and chewing his fingernails, already down to the quick and bleeding. He told Jeb he was hungry, which Jeb took to be a good sign. Back home in Kentucky, Jeb's mom had one cure for most every ailment—buttermilk fried chicken—so Jeb hitched a ride into town and brought back some fried chicken from a fast-food chain. It didn't stay down long— perhaps the Canadian fast-food substitute didn't have the efficacy of his mother's. But Dan did eventually fall asleep, still trembling and kicking.

Jeb cleaned up the last round of puke from the floor, and then ate the remaining fried chicken out of the van's cooler. At least things were going well for Pete, Jeb thought, imagining Pete and Lydia sharing a bottle of wine over a much more refined meal than cold fried chicken. It made him smile. *Good old Stinky Pete,* Jeb thought, *what a guy.* He grabbed his ukulele from the crate under the bed, then sat down in the open van door and began to play.

The wind pushed the tinny notes of the ukulele through the spruce trees, where they were quickly lost to the sonic vacuum of the forest. The mossy boulders and fuzzy pines created an anechoic environment where sounds were as muted as the green and brown colors of the vegetation. The air was turning cool from a building storm and the oncoming darkness. Fall is the season of change, and it was on the way.

***

Pete dried himself with a towel on the shore of Alice Lake, which sat in a slight depression just north of town surrounded by pine-covered hills. The lake had an official swimming beach, but Pete and Lydia had chosen their own shore, far from anyone else. The water in the lake was quite cold, even at the end of summer. Pete thought that Lydia's northern upbringing must have made her immune to the frigid temperatures, given that she was still swimming. He slipped into his clothes and sat down in the grass. He'd been trying to find the courage to tell Lydia about the drugs and money, but now that everything seemed to be going so well between them, he wasn't sure if he should.

"What's the matter there, loverboy?" Lydia called out to him while she treaded water. "Looks like Private Willy retreated back to the barracks!"

Pete shook his head and smiled. He was getting used to her crude humor again, but he still blushed. "Are you almost done in there? I'm getting hungry."

"Yep, clean as I ever am. It's not even that cold." Lydia said, slowly making her way back to shore. "Nipples as hard as marbles though!"

Pete brought her towel to her as she emerged from the water. He averted his gaze, although Lydia was not terribly quick to cover herself. Once clothed, she sat down on the shore and grabbed two beers out of her backpack, pitching one to Pete.

"I thought we were heading to dinner," asked Pete, cracking the beer anyway.

"We're having dinner here. I brought sandwiches," she said. "This spot is prettier than any restaurant in town. Should be a good sunset."

"Pretty killer day, right? What do you think we climbed, 10 pitches? I think *Steve's Little Secret* was my favorite. Then a swim and some dinner. Perfection." He paused. "Lydia, I don't want this to end."

He immediately regretted his words. He'd gotten caught in the moment, and now he was afraid that he would push Lydia away again. He looked over at her, trying to see her reaction, waiting for her to speak.

"I don't either, Pete," she said, matching his gaze. "I want to come with you when you leave."

Pete couldn't hide his excitement. He smiled, but he couldn't think of what to say.

"I mean, if that's OK?" It was Lydia's turn to be nervous.

"Yeah, of course! That would be...amazing," he stammered.

"The coffee shop is doing so well that I can afford to hire a manager. And I'm tired of the cold-ass winters up here."

Pete looked down at the ground, feeling deflated by her explanation. He had hoped, of course, that her motivation was entirely emotional.

"And I want to be with you," she said finally, almost disappointed in herself for her sentiment. She scooted closer to Pete and put her arm across his shoulders.

"Awesome," Pete said, relieved. "Lydia, I think that I..." He paused, reconsidering his words. "I think that I'm pretty hungry. Let's get into those sandwiches."

***

The fog hung low over Howe sound long after the sun had risen. Soon the air would warm and the fog would dissolve back to transparency, but for now the misty clouds suited Dan's mood. He had woken up long before Jeb, feeling decidedly well considering his state the mornings before. He hadn't left the van much for the past three days, so Jeb was surprised to find him smoking a cigarette and drinking a cup of coffee in the grassy, sunlit meadow below the van.

"Hey man," said Jeb, studying Dan for any indications of his health. "Don't you look like a bouquet of flowers this morning," he said, sitting down next to him.

"Feeling pretty good, actually," said Dan, taking a drag. "Thanks for taking care of me this week, means the world."

"For you, man—anything. You really are looking better." Jeb put his arm around Dan and patted his shoulder.

"I feel good enough to climb, I think. Wanna go?"

Jeb had his doubts. "Really? I guess we could go do something mellow, huh?"

"What about *Mary's Merkin*? I've heard its good."

"What? You are coming off of heroin, haven't climbed forever, and you want to go do the infamous *Merkin*—the guidebook says it's the scariest *five-nine* you will ever climb." Jeb was incredulous. "Why don't we go boulder a bit instead? Much more mellow."

"If you knew the shit I'd been through since the last time you saw me, it wouldn't seem crazy at all. I'll lead the scary pitch; it would be good to feel a little fear again. I've been numb for so long that any emotion sounds refreshing." Dan took a slow sip of coffee, then looked at Jeb intently.

"I've been sitting around, not doing shit other than shooting up for a long time. Just hanging out waiting to die, really. Time to start living again, my man." Dan snuffed out his cigarette and got up out of his chair. "Look, I've still got two legs and two arms," he said shaking his appendages, "and apparently more guts than you." Dan laughed. "Drink some coffee and grab your gear. And try to keep up. I got too much living to make up for to be waiting around." Dan shot Jeb a sly smile as he headed back to the van to rack up.

***

On Chen's command, Hulin kicked open the door to Dan's Pender street apartment. It hadn't taken Chen long to find the address, as Dan's associates in the Triad showed very little loyalty while facing Chen's threats of violence. Hulin entered first, gun drawn. Dan's roommate Julian was on the couch gaming, just as Dan had left him days ago. The lights were off in the house, but the glowing TV softly illuminated the smoke rising from a recently used water bong on the coffee table. Through the smoke, Julian's face showed no sign of surprise, as if it was every day that two Chinese men in black suits kicked open his front door.

"Whoa, man," said Julian. "What's the big fucking deal?"

Hulin jumped over the coffee table and smashed Julian's face with the side of his gun. "Where is Dan?" he shouted.

Julian tried to shake off the blow, suddenly realizing the seriousness of the situation. "He's not here. Haven't seen him for days."

Chen stepped through the door. "Search the place," he said, motioning to Hulin. Then he pointed his gun at Julian. "Tell us where Dan is, or I will kill you."

Julian pressed himself back into the couch cushions. He stared at the floor, trying to remember where Dan had said he was going. He looked at Chen, suddenly recalling what Dan had told him before he left.

"He went up north. Packed up a bunch of gear and said he was going climbing in Squamish." Julian looked pleased with himself for remembering.

"Thanks," said Chen, pulling the trigger.

CHAPTER TWENTY-FIVE

Jeb had offered to buy everyone beers to celebrate Dan's return to climbing, so after dinner the four set off to the Twisted Snag. Jeb, Pete, and Lydia were inside ordering another round while Dan stepped outside for a cigarette. He had decided to quit drinking as long as he was quitting substances, but so far cigarettes were proving too difficult to kick. He zipped up his down jacket and dug in its pocket for his beanie—the fall evenings were starting to get cold. Tourist season was trickling to an end and the streets of Squamish were empty. Dan smoked his cigarette and watched the stoplight cycle through its colors without any cars passing through. After the third cycle, he laughed out loud. Perhaps it was Dan's new lease on life, but he found the scene poetic and somehow relevant to his own life. It was as if he, like the stop lights, was just going through the motions without much awareness of the world around him. But at least he had enough clarity to recognize it and laugh. He felt good—his body seemed to be normalizing, he was surrounded by friends for the first time in years, and climbing again felt like falling in love for the first time.

Dan watched a sleek sports car pull into the hotel parking lot across the street, and immediately recognized it as Chen's. His stomach knotted. He stepped back into the shadows and watched Chen and Hulin enter the hotel lobby. The BMW's lights flashed twice as Chen locked the doors. He tossed his cigarette and went back inside the bar.

"We need to leave," Dan said to Jeb upon returning inside.

"Ah man, you're less fun now that you're not drinking. We

just ordered another round."

Dan interrupted Pete and Lydia's conversation bluntly and motioned for Jeb to huddle closer. "We're in trouble. Just saw a couple of the Hóng Lóng outside, they are here for me. And you've all been seen around town with me, which puts you in danger too." Dan looked at each person trying to judge their reaction but was only met by blank stares. Lydia looked especially confused. "We need to leave by morning. We don't have to go together, but we need to go."

The group exchanged confused looks. Jeb was the first to break the silence.

"I think we should stick together. Dan, no offense, but you're not fully stable yet. Plus, I didn't nurse you back from death just to have you killed by gangsters." Jeb smiled but his humor was lost on the rest. "Pete and Lydia here have been talking about going back to Ten Sleep for the fall."

Jeb's statement was once again met with silence. "Plan?" he asked, looking around at his friends for confirmation.

Dan nodded. "Ten Sleep it is."

***

Late in the evening as Jeb lay asleep in the van, Dan took the cash he had received from Chen back out from its hiding spot under the spare-wheel well and pushed it into his backpack. They couldn't afford to attempt to cross the border with the money—Jeb and Pete had already pushed their luck at border crossings, and from their story the border agents would treat them with extra scrutiny on their return. They didn't understand the Triad and what they were capable of. If Chen were to catch up with them, the money was only a liability. He might kill them even without the cash, but certainly would with it. He knew a spot to hide it, a deep granite crevice he had once stumbled upon while climbing high on top of the Chief. Far from any trail, a place that only lost climbers would ever find—it would be safe. Dan was sure that Jeb and Pete would understand when the time came.

Dan sat in the dark, thinking. He hoped that he was transitioning between the worst times of his life onto something else; hopefully better, but at least different. In between the darkness and the unknown, a prayer seemed appropriate, even if he wasn't sure how to pray or to whom. He did the only thing that seemed approximately correct and assumed a pose he had done once in yoga while vocalizing his repentance of the past and his hopes for the time to come. He put a water bottle and climbing shoes in the backpack with the money and seated a headlamp on his head, then pulled the laces of his running shoes tight and tied them. It was going to be a long night.

***

Chen pulled off of Highway 99 just outside Surrey when it became clear that Dan and his friends were planning to cross the border. He and Hulin did not have their passports, real or forged, and they had a trunk full of guns—neither of which would allow safe passage into the U.S. It would be more prudent, if indeed they decided to pursue their prey, to return to base and regroup. Chen had a multitude of passports to choose from, and weapons were easier to borrow from their alliances in Seattle than to smuggle across. Maybe he would trade the BMW for his new motorhome and enjoy the chase in luxury? Time was not of the essence as they were confident as to where they might find the van and its crew, thanks to the words the red-headed girl had written in the dust on the back window as they fueled up at the last gas station:

Ten Sleep or Bust!

Chapter Twenty-Six

An afternoon thunderstorm rolled through the Bighorn Basin as if it were on tracks, prompting Burl to cut his gardening session short. It was important to him to keep his wife's irises alive since her passing, a sometimes precarious effort through the years. He decided to drive into Worland for a late lunch— the pastrami sandwich at the Bighorn Cafe was always worth the extra drive, as compared to having *yet another* cheeseburger at the Two Bit. A few miles from town, Burl felt his pager buzz and took a quick look after he rounded a shallow curve. Sheriff Dawes generally didn't bother him on his day off, so Burl knew it was important enough to justify stopping by the office. He continued down the road toward Worland, his stomach protesting his plan for a short detour. The incoming storm blew plumes of red sand across the road as Burl pulled into the sheriff's office parking lot. He parked and went inside.

"Afternoon, sheriff. What can I do for you today?" said Burl as he stepped into the office.

Frank was surprised to see him. He pulled his reading glasses from his face and ran a hand over his buzz-cut grey hair. "Didn't mean for you to come in on your day off, I was just hoping to talk to you over the phone."

Burl shut the door and sat down on the torn leather couch in Frank's office, the major holes patched with duct tape. "I was coming into town anyway, figured I'd stop in. What's going on?"

"Always good to talk in person. I got an interesting call from the DEA's office in Denver. Sounds like they have an interest in rolling over the hill and poking around a bit. They wouldn't tell me much, but I'm sure they got their reasons." Frank cracked his knuckles into his palm, then grabbed his coffee mug off the desk. "I gave them clearance, and I told them to come talk to you in case it was related to Lyle in any way. I figured you wouldn't mind a little help, being as it doesn't seem like there has been much progress on that one." Frank looked at Burl with raised eyebrows.

Burl could feel his chest constrict as his pulse quickened. Frank was a decade younger than Burl, and while he could usually swallow his pride and obey the sheriff's direction, he did not appreciate the insinuation.

"Well, it's a tough case. Not much to go on. But there has been some progress. I was…"

Frank interrupted, "I was not implying that you aren't doing everything you can, Burl. I understand that this has been difficult. Just talk to the Feds when they come, see what they have to say. They will be here Tuesday, first thing in the morning."

Burl swallowed and nodded his head at Frank. "I'll be there. Thanks for the help."

***

Burl knew he should've left the Two Bit after his self-imposed two beer limit, but tonight his frustrations pushed his normal discipline into rapid retreat. He was out of ideas in his investigation. He missed Lyle. He couldn't escape the thought that Ten Sleep was no longer the place it used to be. On top of it all, he was lonely. Burl told himself a few extra pints would shake loose new ideas about the murder or mask some of his longing, but now he just liked the feeling of being drunk again. He slid his pint glass in circles, seeing how high he could get the remaining beer up its side.

"Are you fucking Monty?" Burl asked suddenly, his speech slow and hoarse.

The question stopped Sunny on her path to the cash register. She turned around and took a few steps back toward Burl, crossing her arms as she walked.

"What did you say? It better not be what I thought I just heard." She spoke quietly so that the other bar patrons couldn't hear. Sunny had noted that he consumed more than his usual but hadn't noticed that he was drunk when she poured him the beer he was currently finishing. The cigarette he asked to borrow should have been a clue.

"Sunny, I just can't figure it out. I'm at the end of my line here. Nothing makes sense."

"What are you talking about? Why would you think that I was, uh, sleeping with Monty?" Sunny's anger was partially replaced with concern.

"Motive, my dear." Burl closed his eyes and shook his head in a condescending manner. "At the root of every crime is a motive to commit one." He looked pleased with his explanation.

"Monty did not kill Lyle. Burl, you're drunk. You should go home." Her voice was much softer now.

"Why would you defend him so quickly?" Burl slurred slightly. "Don't you want to find out who murdered your husband?" He slapped the bar as he finished his sentence.

Sunny looked down the bar to see if anyone at the bar was taking notice of Burl's outburst. "Burl, please be quiet." She leaned in close to him, whispering. "I don't know who killed Lyle, but it wasn't Monty. Despite what you might have heard—I've heard those rumors too—Monty had no reason to kill Lyle." She backed away and swung a bar rag over her shoulder. "Besides, I don't think Monty could hit the broadside of a barn. You can move a man from the city to the country and stick a hat on his head, but that don't make him a cowboy."

"Folks like him are the problem with this place," Burl muttered under his breath.

"What's that? You're slurring."

"Nothing," he said, waving off the comment with his hand. "I've tried to do good, Sunny. The world just doesn't seem to let me." Burl stared at himself in the bar mirror as Sunny stood silent, not sure how to respond. He laid his head down on his arms, crossed on top of the bar, and shut his eyes.

Sunny let out a sigh, putting her hands in her back pockets as she shook her head. "Get up, Burl. I'll give you a ride home."

Sunny locked arms with Burl and led him through the door, walking better than she expected. They turned the corner onto the side street where Sunny's car was parked, pausing as she dug into her purse for her keys. Burl looked over the top of her car at the yard across the street. He started laughing.

"It's the gawd-damn horse." Burl turned to Sunny in amazement. He shuffled around the car and crossed the street. A painted mare was standing in the yard with its head down in the lawn, eating grass, a loose lead rope hanging from its bridle. Burl approached carefully.

"Hey girl," he whispered.

"Whatchya doing over there?" Sunny yelled from across the street.

Burl turned to Sunny and held a finger in front of his mouth. He took another step toward the horse and grabbed the lead rope. He led the horse to a large planter pot in the corner of the yard. Burl stepped into the center of the planter, smashing the marigolds inside with his boot. He threw his other leg over the horse, pulling himself onto its back with an arm wrapped over its neck. The planter fell over on its side, soil spilling out onto the lawn. Burl steadied himself and sat upright.

"I found my horse Sunny!" Burl yelled, a smile wrapping his face. He prodded the horse with his boot heels, leaving Sunny staring as he rode down the street.

***

Burl woke up late, his head foggy from the night before. After getting out of bed and putting his robe and slippers on, he stumbled to the kitchen to make coffee. He tried to recall his conversation with Sunny, but the details escaped him. He knew the topic and the tone, and that he probably said at least a few things he should regret. Burl filled up the coffee maker with water, looking out the window over the sink. Tied to the small crab apple tree in his front yard was a paint horse, its tail and mane full of cockleburs. He rubbed his eyes and blinked slowly. It was Cole's lost horse, the distinctive brown and white spot pattern matching the description.
"I'll be damned." Burl said, making his way outside, still carrying the coffee pot. *Somebody must be fucking with me. Is it a taunt? Is someone rubbing my face in my failure?* He stood in the yard in his robe and slippers, scratching the horse's face, trying to figure out the meaning of it all.

***

"Morning, Sunny. It's Burl." He was standing in the kitchen with a cup of coffee in one hand, phone in the other, staring out the window at the horse.

"Morning? It's damn near noon." Sunny's tone was dry.

"I'm really sorry about last night. Had a bit too much to drink—not blaming you—and ran my mouth. Said some things I ought not have."

114

The line was silent. Burl waited until it was clear that she wasn't going to reply.

"OK, understandable. I'll let you go. Sorry again."

Sunny spoke just as Burl was moving the phone from his ear.

"It's alright, Burl. We're not ourselves right now, with everything that has happened. I'm not mad. Never seen you that drunk. Bet you got a bit of a ringer this morning, huh?"

"I've felt better. Thanks for not being too upset."

"How was that horse ride last night anyway? Looked like you were about to fall off for as long as I could see. Guess you survived."

"What ride?"

"You don't remember?"

"Nothing about a horse." He could hear Sunny laughing as he spoke.

"I walked you out of the bar to give you a ride home. There was a horse loose across the street in Roger's yard. Before I knew it, you were riding her home. I laughed my ass off at you slumped over her neck, plodding down the street."

"Where did the horse come from?" asked Burl.

"Hell if I know. By all the burrs in her tail, it looked like she had been loose for a while."

Burl hung up the phone. He could almost hear the universe laughing at him.

***

Up until last night, it had been decades since Burl had reason or desire to ride a horse. He secretly hated horses, having been thrown off more than one. He preferred his quad for traveling off-road, but disliking horses wasn't something a person admitted to in Wyoming—better to say you prefer kombucha to Coors or bicycling to bull riding.

Cole hadn't answered his phone, but Burl decided to drive the horse to his place regardless. With the horse lead now a dead end, he was anxious to get back to following up on the Fingers gang after his encounter a few days ago. He had rummaged around the warehouse after he was sure that the perpetrators were gone, but the search yielded very little information. The encounter hung in Burl's mind. He wondered what he could have done differently, if he was too old and scared to be a good deputy anymore. With a little more evidence, maybe he could just hand over the investigation to the feds from Denver.

Burl turned the truck and trailer onto Cole's driveway, drove down to its end and parked near the farmhouse. He walked over to the door and knocked, but no one answered. Burl looked around, spotting the horse barn. He walked back to the trailer, untied the lead rope, and led the horse over to the barn. Inside, the barn was strangely quiet. Burl led the horse past several open stalls. He kept walking to the end of the alley, finding all of the stalls empty. *I hope Cole sells more tomatoes than horses*, thought Burl. He walked back closer to the front and put the horse in a stall. He tossed in a slab of hay and scratched the mare's face from over the stall gate. "You're a pretty good girl—for a horse." Burl said in a soothing voice. He pulled a hose from the spigot in the center alley and filled up the stall's water trough. "If Cole isn't home by tomorrow, I'll come back by and give you some more."

Burl left the barn and walked back toward his truck, pausing as he approached the driver's side door. After a moment of thought, he turned and walked over to the nearest greenhouse.

Inside, Burl was again surprised—the greenhouse was as empty as the horse barn. *I thought hothouse tomatoes grew year-round,* thought Burl. *I guess I know as much about tomatoes as cutting horses.* He walked down the center aisle of tables. From the standing water on the ground, and the moist soil on the tables, it appeared that the greenhouse had been in use recently. *Maybe it's harvest time for tomatoes on top of sugar beets.* He bent over and picked up a flower petal from the dirt, bright scarlet in color, inspecting it before tossing it back on the ground.

***

Peering out between window curtains, Cole watched Burl enter the horse barn. He took a small step back from the window and crossed his arms. In the few days since the disaster in Denver, he'd been debating what to do about the deputy, wondering how much he might know. Burl's presence here might force his hand. As Burl walked out from the barn, Cole leaned in behind the window frame to ensure his silhouette couldn't be seen from outside. He watched Burl leave the barn and walk over to his truck, then turn around and enter a greenhouse. Cole stepped back to the window. He was breathing heavier now, a bead of sweat gathering on his brow. His mind stopped debating the details of his situation—he was back in battle. He watched Burl leave the greenhouse and get in his truck. Cole relaxed the grip on his pistol as Burl's truck disappeared down the drive.

Chapter Twenty-Seven

One swig of cold coffee, and one swig of Old Milwaukee—Java stout baby! You've got to try it."

Jeb passed the steel mug over to Lydia, who already had an open can of beer between her knees. She took a sip of her beer and held it in her mouth as she added a bit of coffee from Jeb's mug. She was halfway through swallowing when it came flying back out of her mouth in an exaggerated manner.

"Instant coffee? You fucking heathen! I knew there was something I didn't trust about you." Lydia yelled at Jeb with mock seriousness.

Pete laughed from behind the wheel of the van. "You can detect instant coffee with a mouth full of shitty beer? My, what a proper lady you are."

"Hey—remember my profession. Bad coffee is an insult to my craft. It's like if Jeb here was replaced by...." Lydia, for once, stumbled over her words. "It's like if Pete got..." she paused again. "You guys don't even have jobs, much less crafts, damn lowbaggers. You have no idea what I'm talking about." Lydia thought briefly then smiled. "It's like if Dan got replaced by a heroin vending machine. It takes away all pride and heritage of a practice." She kicked the back of Dan's seat in front of her to let him know she wasn't serious. "Just kidding, Danimal. I still can't believe the crazy shit you boys have gotten yourself into. Drugs, money, Yakuza. What the fuck."

"Triads," Dan corrected, "You call them Yakuza and it would be the last word you spoke."

Lydia grimaced. "You really have no idea what these guys

want from you? Can't think of anything that might have pissed them off?"

"As far as I know, the deal I made them with Jeb and Pete's heroin should have repaid my debts. I gave them a half million worth of dope for 200 grand. More than enough. But you can't trust these guys—I bet they were trying to steal the money back."

"What do we do now?" Lydia asked.

"A couple of months to let them cool off and move on to other matters, and they won't even remember it—it's not that much money to them. Then we go back up to Squamish and get the money."

"And then we get paaaa-iiiid!" interrupted Jeb.

"You sound overly excited for someone who is only going to buy gas, noodles, and cheap beer with his windfall. You're the cheapest person I've ever met," teased Lydia.

"She's right, Jeb," said Pete. "I should know better than anyone. Hell, on the way up to Squamish he made soup at a gas station with the free hot water and ketchup rather than pay two bucks for a corn dog."

"Don't knock the hustle," said Jeb. "The less I spend, the less I work. Simple as that. Besides, I wouldn't pollute this temple with a truck-stop corn dog." Jeb motioned across his body.

"Temple, my ass." laughed Dan. "I once saw you grab unfinished plates back out of the dish bin at Yosemite Lodge-kid's plates even, all mashed up and properly snotted."

"OK, enough. Hate the game, not the player," said Jeb. "Now, let's talk some more about our so-called plan."

"Super simple, for those who were sleeping the first time we went over it," Pete looked behind him toward Jeb. "Climb at Ten Sleep until the weather starts to turn bad and things cool off with Dan's situation. Dan goes back to Squamish, gets the money, magically gets it across the border to us, and then we caravan to Potrero Chico via Hueco Tanks."

"It's the magic part that worries me," Jeb said, agitated.

"You will get your money," said Dan. "I have my ways."

Jeb nodded. "I'll trust you on this one. You know more about the underworld than the rest of us. Obviously. Anyone want to split another Java Stout with me?"

Chapter Twenty-Eight

Gordon was too agitated to properly concentrate, so he placed a pinch of chewing tobacco in his lip and paced through the sugar mill. He'd tried to convince Cole that the climbers had the heroin and that he could find them, but Cole wouldn't listen. It was a foolish hope to find two climbers living in a van anywhere in the West—Gordon couldn't remember the name of the place they were headed, but the task would have been much more exciting than preparing the mill for harvest or boiling down a load of opium sap. Part of Gordon's unrest was his instinct that he and Cole should halt production until things settled down in the county, but Cole vetoed that idea as well.

Gordon spit in a styrofoam Maverik cup and walked through the main boiler room, the wooden plank floor creaking as he approached the small side room where his poppy sludge was waiting. The stew gave off a distinct odor, but Gordon didn't mind. Just as with the foul stink of sugar beets boiling or moonshine distilling, it smelled like money. Gordon smiled at his progress. A few more processing steps and he could pass the mess off to Cole to finish. The last steps were the dangerous ones, as the volatile mixture was prone to explode, and he wasn't going to risk blowing himself up if Cole so quickly volunteered to do the dangerous work. Gordon thought that Cole might secretly like the danger, as if he missed the thrill from his time overseas.

Gordon pulled the flashlight from its holster on his belt and peered into the bottom of the industrial kettle. The solutes had properly settled out overnight, the remaining liquid was now mostly transparent. Gordon turned the heat to the kettle back on and grabbed the ethanol and charcoal mixture from the shelf, pouring it into the kettle until the container was empty. Gordon tried to remember the term that old moonshiners used when adding charcoal to smooth out the flavor of their whiskey, wondering if the charcoal in Cole's recipe had a similar effect. It seemed like his memory was deteriorating as fast as his body.

"Polish," Gordon muttered to himself as he slid the mesh cover back on the kettle. "It's called a polish." He turned off the lights to the room and locked the door behind him. He sang a rhyme to himself as he walked down the hall with a bouncy cadence, proud his memory still occasionally functioned and excited to be done with his portion of the refinement process. "Polish, astonish, Amish, snobbish…" He stopped suddenly, the rhyme jarring loose a memory he had been trying to retrieve for days. *"Squamish,"* he said out loud, grinning broadly. "They were headed to Squamish." He spit the tobacco wad from his lip onto the floor, his pace quickening toward the exit.

Chapter Twenty-Nine

Burl sat in his office chair, nervously twirling a pen between his fingers as he waited for Agent Springer to arrive. He had finished cleaning up his cluttered desk, arranging the assorted papers into tidy stacks, but now wondered if it looked too tidy. He reached for a stack and fanned them out slightly. Better. He walked over to this bookshelf by the door and blew a bit of dust off the books and assortment of knick-knacks gathered in front. He straightened the picture on the wall next to the bookshelf. Back at his desk, he decided that the fan of papers looked too intentional and gathered them up in a neat stack again.

A knock came at the door, which then opened enough for Henry Springer to lean his head in.

"Deputy Hutchinson?"

"Ah, hello Agent Springer. Come on in."

He walked in and extended his hand toward Burl. "Please, call me Hank."

Burl smiled and motioned at the chair. "Thanks for coming by. Have a seat."

"Thanks," he said, sitting down. "I appreciate your time. As you know, I've been briefed of your progress by Sheriff Dawes." He looked up at Burl, a more serious expression on his face. "I take it that the Sheriff doesn't know about your encounter with the Fingers down in Denver?"

Burl was noticeably surprised by the question. "Uh, yes, correct." He looked up at agent Springer nervously.

"I figured. No problem, it can stay between us." He offered Burl a faint smile.

"How'd you know?"

Hank winked. "We've been watching them, too."

Burl shuffled in his seat. "I, uh, was—am—a little embarrassed by that incident. And a bit out of my jurisdiction."

"If it makes you feel better, we think your instinct was right. Satan's Fingers have a connection up here—a supplier most likely. We've suspected this for some time, but we don't have any hard evidence. My question for you is what led you to Denver? What's the connection to the Fingers?"

Burl looked down at his desk and considered his response. "To be honest with you, I went to Denver out of desperation. Don't have many leads on this murder investigation, so I have been swinging pretty wide if you know what I mean. Lots of strikeouts." Burl laughed softly. "I got a tip from a local here about a truck parked in the victim's neighborhood a few times recently, Colorado plates and a Satan's Fingers sticker on the back window. It's embarrassing, really, that I acted on it. Not what you would call a solid lead, right?"

Hank nodded. "And the victim? Any reason to think he was involved with Satan's Fingers?"

Burl shook his head. "Don't think so. Lyle lived pretty clean."

"What did he do for a living?" Hank had his pen pressed to the notebook in his lap but had yet to write anything down.

"Lots of things, jack-of-all-trades I suppose. Most recently he was trucking cutting horses around. Auctions, mostly, if I understand it correctly."

"OK, thanks." The agent wrote a few notes. "Any other events or people around Ten Sleep that you think might be connected to the Fingers?"

"Nah. We got a few Harley aficionados around, but no one that does anything gang related. Mostly riding and wrenchin'— the Harley way, right?" Burl chuckled. "Wish I had more for you. This murder case has nothing but dead ends so far."

"Thanks, Deputy. You've given me what I need. Don't take this the wrong way, but my interest is pinning Satan's Fingers with federal interstate transport of narcotics and racketeering, not your murder case. And please, try to stay away from the Fingers from here on out, I don't want you to tip them off any more than you might have already." The agent stood up and put his notebook back in his jacket pocket.

Burl swallowed, trying to comprehend the agent's last statement. "Yes, sir." He reached his open hand towards Hank.

"If you do happen along anything related, I trust you'll send it my way?"

Hank shook Burl's hand. "Of course. Hopefully we can help each other out in some manner or another."

He walked towards the office door, paused briefly at the bookcase and bent slightly to examine Lyle's Folsom point that Burl had on the shelf. "Say, that's a cool arrowhead. Did you find that around here?"

"It's too big to be an arrowhead, don't you think?" Burl laughed. "It's a spear point. And I didn't find it. It was a…gift." Burl paused uncomfortably. He stood up and walked over to Hank. "It's a beauty, though. Very rare. I've found a few spear points before, but only practice points I reckon."

"What's a practice point?" asked Hank, still inspecting the spearhead.

Burl put his hands on his hips. "Only a theory, really. These points took a lot of time to make and must have broken quite often given how brittle they are and how many shards of them people seem to find. And throwing a spear accurately isn't easy. I think these hunters practiced throwing spears and made points specifically to do so. Unfinished, crudely made ones. No way of knowing for sure, of course. Lots of people don't think these hunters were smart enough to practice anything."

Agent Springer straightened back up from the bookshelf. "That seems like a pretty sound theory. I'm not a hunter, but before I went on a hunt it sure seems like I would take a few shots from my rifle beforehand." He smiled and patted the gun holster at his side, "The sidearm is another story. I keep damn sharp on this thing; go to the range almost every week," the agent said, winking at Burl. "Well, better be on my way."

Hank turned and exited the door. Burl stood, hands still on his hips, thinking.

CHAPTER THIRTY

How do you like driving my dream machine, Hulin?" yelled Chen from the back bed of his motorhome, his head momentarily lifting from the pillow as he spoke. A quick nap had elevated his spirits immensely.

Hulin turned his head slightly and lowered the volume of the satellite radio. "Very nice, Master Chen. It's smooth."

Chen's head returned to the pillow and he shut his eyes again. "Maybe on the way home we can stop and spend a few nights in Yellowstone. I've heard it's beautiful."

"I'd like that," Hulin said, lying. He had objected earlier to taking the motorhome on this trip. It was too conspicuous and slow for their mission, but Chen insisted. Hulin also didn't think that he would enjoy camping, but he didn't feel like he could object, and Chen was obviously enamored by his new motorhome.

"Hulin, how much diesel do we have? It seems we've been driving forever." Chen sat up on the bed, admiring the mountain range out the right window.

Hulin looked down at the dash, suddenly worried. "Running low, boss."

Chen got up quickly and rushed forward to the passenger seat. He glanced at the dash, then started pressing buttons on the built-in navigator screen.

"Ah, lucky for you, Hulin. There is a gas station coming up soon. Otherwise you might be pushing!" Chen laughed. "Take exit 195, don't miss it." Chen pressed a few more buttons before leaning back into the seat. "This is Montana, huh? I thought there might be snow."

Hulin nodded, not having any notion as to whether snow should be expected this early in the year. At the exit, he eased the motorhome off the interstate and into the gas station, pulling up to an unoccupied diesel pump. Hulin shut off the engine. "Need a snack, boss? I'm going to go in to get a soda."

"Get me some chicken strips if they have some, that would be great." Chen was excited by the idea of a snack, suddenly realizing how hungry he had become. He got out of the passenger side door and inserted his credit card into the pump. After the nozzle was inserted and the pump running, he proceeded to scrub and squeegee the windshield, working carefully not to allow the cleaning fluid to drip on the vehicle's shiny black paint. As he walked back to return the squeegee to its reservoir, he spotted a familiar van leaving the gas station—Dan's van, the writing still present in the dust on the back window. He froze, his mind racing. The squeegee slipped from his hand onto the concrete.

"Hulin!" Chen yelled as he hurried back to the pump, squeezing the nozzle lever harder in hopes the fuel might come out faster. The climber's van turned onto the interstate ramp and accelerated as he watched, helpless to pursue. He turned toward the store entrance, scanning the exterior windows for signs of Hulin, who was just reaching the checkout. Chen waved his free arm up and down frantically, mouthing "Let's go!" with exaggerated motions. Hulin raised a hand up and shrugged in confusion before understanding the gesture and running outside, clutching a soda and a paper basket of fried chicken.

***

Gordon's foot relaxed off the accelerator every time his mind wandered, causing him to lose precious time on his planned 18-hour drive to Squamish. He was less than halfway there, with Montana's Pioneer range shrinking in his rearview mirror like a miniature diorama and had every reason to hurry. As confident as he was in the climber's destination, he didn't know how long they would be there and worse, he hadn't told Cole of his plan. It was a situation where asking for forgiveness clearly rivaled asking for permission, especially if his hunt was successful. He pressed the accelerator as he tried to clear his mind.

His phone buzzed against the dashboard, but Gordon hesitated to pick it up. There was only one person that ever called him, and he had hoped that Cole wouldn't have bothered him for a few more days.

"Yeah, what is it?" Gordon asked hesitantly as he finally picked up his phone.

"Trouble." Cole's tone was flat but clear. "The deputy was nosing around my place yesterday. I think he knows. Need you to come over so we can talk it through."

"OK. What time tomorrow works for you?" Gordon was already slowing down his truck.

"Tonight. We better move quickly on this."

"Can't do tonight, I'm afraid. I'm up the road a bit." Gordon scanned the horizon for the next exit. He had no plans to tell Cole that he had embarked on this mission.

"Alright. Come by tomorrow afternoon, anytime."

Gordon hung up his phone and tossed it back on the dashboard. He eased the truck down the off-ramp, pulling through the interstate underpass to the interchange on the other side. He decided to fill up on fuel before the long trip back to Ten Sleep. He pulled into the pump behind a gleaming black motorhome and started filling up.

"You 'bout done with that?" Gordon asked the Asian man in front of him, who was seemingly washing every window in his RV with the only squeegee at the pump. The man ignored his question.

Gordon saw an orange Econoline pulling out of the gas station. It was unmistakably the climbers' van, stickers covering the back doors, duffle bags lashed to the roof rack. "I'll be dipped in shit," he muttered as he scrambled to the gas pump, pulling the nozzle out and dropping it on the ground. He slid into the driver's seat and sped off.

Chapter Thirty-One

The crew was packed tight in the Econoline with Pete at the wheel. It might have been today's weed or last night's whiskey, but Lydia was no longer feeling confident of the group's trajectory.

"Do you guys still think this is a good plan?" she said, talking fast. "I think Lander or Spearfish might be better places to lay low. Any news on the dead guy? If he was local, somebody in the area probably knows what he was carrying. What if someone could connect you to it?"

Jeb shook his head. "Not a chance. We were all alone that night, the only people that know about it are in this van. I don't know anything more about the accident, but I haven't been reading the Worland Daily News too often either." Jeb smirked. "Besides, Pete and I got our *projects* in Ten Sleep, Lydia—projects. Routes left unsent. You know their pull."

Lydia didn't seem appeased. "No, I really don't. Meaningless goals. A waste of time. And what about the Yakuza—I mean the Triads—you're sure they couldn't have followed us?"

"Better to call them Jacuzzi than Yakuza..." started Jeb, a grin hanging on his face. "But either way you are in hot water!" Jeb chuckled and looked around, but he was the only one laughing.

"Good one, knucklehead." Dan said. "But no, there is no way. We got out of there clean." Dan, unlike Lydia, was feeling better than he had for a long time. "Besides, do *you* even know where we are? Myself, I got lost somewhere between the old copper smelter, Pete's boring-ass story about Iranians first cultivating alfalfa, and those wooden things he called *beaverslides*, whatever the fuck they are. Welcome to Montana, eh Pete?"

Pete barely managed a smile. "It's still the closest thing to home that I have, outside of this van I suppose. Tallest smelter in the world, if you can believe it. And beaverslides are for stacking hay. Doesn't rot stacked like it does in bales. Don't get me started on alfalfa."

"Beaver Slide? Gonna put that on the list of potential new route names." Jeb laughed as Lydia rolled her eyes.

"Would anyone mind if we stopped by my folks' house for the night? They would be pissed if they found out I drove by without stopping. We could get showers and a free home-cooked meal." Pete seemed to be trying to sell the proposal.

"Hell yeah, Skinny. I would love to meet the fine people that spawned a character such as yourself. And Dan certainly could use a shower." Jeb raised an eyebrow.

"This isn't some *meet the parents* bullshit, is it Petey?" asked Lydia. "Not into it."

Pete knew that Lydia wasn't completely serious with her comment, but it startled him anyway. "No, I promise it's not that. If it makes you more comfortable, I'll introduce you as just part of the crew. Not my…girlfriend." It sounded more like a question than a statement. He looked at Lydia for a response but couldn't find any clues in her face. "Great. Dinner with the family it is. Exit's ten miles ahead."

***

"Great story, Mr. Corbet. That must have been quite an embarrassing moment at the sawmill, huh?"

Pete's father George was reluctantly finishing a tale from his younger days, urged on by Jeb, as they finished up dinner. It was a tight squeeze to fit everyone around the table in the old farmhouse.

"I was never wild and crazy like y'all, but I had my adventures." He grabbed his can of soda and nodded it towards Jeb and Dan, seated across the dining table. His red suspenders, canvas pants, and flannel shirt were relics of his former career at the nearby lumber mill.

"Lydia has an even more embarrassing story to tell. Heard it just the other day." Jeb smiled wildly, looking at Lydia.

"What story, hoser?" she said, indicting Jeb with her stare.

"You know, the pee story." Jeb winked.

"That's not appropriate dinner conversation, Jeb. Plus, I am sure that Mr. and Mrs. Corbet don't share your juvenile sense of humor."

Jeb didn't let it go. "Tell the Corbet's your pee story! You have to."

Pete's mother Gail nodded. "It's OK, dear. We do enjoy a giggle, and it wouldn't be the first time I've blushed."

Lydia looked embarrassed, a rare expression for her. She lifted her bottle to her mouth and finished it with three large gulps. As she put the empty bottle back on the table, a devilish look overtook her face.

"First off, sometimes I get a little nervous before I climb. Usually, this nervousness manifests itself into a sudden need to, uh, urinate. My friends call it the *nervous pee*." Lydia scanned George and Gail's faces to gauge their initial reaction to determine how much detail the rest of the story would entail. "So I was out climbing ice in the Ghost River Wilderness in Southern Alberta, racking up at the bottom of *The Mystery of Morning Wood*. I had a fancy one-piece hard-shell on that a friend had given me— a little overkill for a day of ice climbing, it was really more of an expedition kit. Regardless, it was my first time climbing in it, and I soon discovered why one-pieces fell out of fashion in the 90's: In order to pee, you have to unzip the entire damn thing." Lydia normally tried to control her Canadian accent when she could, but as she started into her story, her enthusiasm exaggerated it.

"So, harness down first, to the ankles. One-piece unzipped, down to the knees." She mimicked the actions with her arms as she spoke them. "Tights down, panties down, pop a squat." Jeb giggled into his fist. "Of course, I am already pretty chilly at this point. The Albertan wind is blowing snow sideways, and it's minus 10 or so."

George's eyes widened. Lydia laughed, "That's centigrade, you know. Probably 15 degrees on your scale, George. So, of course I didn't know it at the time, but the hood on the one-piece had flopped open between my feet, so when I started peeing..." She met everyone's eyes individual as she paused for effect. "I filled it right up."

The whole table started laughing now. Pete's face was red, his mother's more so.

"But wait, I haven't even gotten to the best part yet. So, I pull all the layers back up in the opposite order. I squirm my arms back into the sleeves of the one-piece, zip it up—no problem.

Then, being a bit chilled, of course, I slide the hood back over my helmet!" Lydia put her hands on her forehead, and then slowly pushed her fingers apart to mimic what happened next.

"Piss everywhere! Dripping down off my helmet, onto my face, down the back of my neck. The pee on my helmet freezes, but I was too busy laughing to notice the little yellow icicles hanging down off its edge."

Laughter erupted—even Pete and his mother couldn't hold back behind their embarrassment, but George was laughing hard enough to have a few tears forming in the corners of his eyes.

As the laughter subsided, Lydia folded her hands back in front of her. "Soooo...that's the pee story." She looked around the table in faked shame.

Dan stood up and cleared his throat, then began gathering a few glasses and plates. "Quite the story, Lydia. Really a great digestif. Mrs. Corbet, thanks for the wonderful meal. Jeb and I will do the dishes."

"Dan, you are quite the gentleman, but Pete and I will get the dishes," Gail replied. "It will give us some time to catch up. Why don't the rest of you take showers, get your sleeping bags settled, maybe watch some TV. It has probably been some time since you've had creature comforts."

As the crew cleared out of the dining room, Gail slipped an apron over her head and tied the back, then rolled up the sleeves on her floral printed blouse. "I'll wash, you dry, just like the old days, right?"

Pete picked up a drying towel from its rack under the counter. "Sure thing, Mom. Thanks again for feeding my friends and letting us all stay here."

"Of course, dear. It is always nice to meet your friends. I really like Lydia. A bit crass, but a girl with a little spunk is good for you."

"It's not like that, Mom. She's a friend." Pete tidied the drying rack in order to avoid eye contact with his mother.

"Whatever you say, Pete." Gail scrubbed another plate before putting it down into the rinse side of the sink. "I think your father got a kick out of the stories your friends told tonight. I know he hasn't always been supportive of your decisions, and thinks you should apply yourself a little more, but I want you to know that we just want you to be happy. No matter what."

Pete smiled sincerely. "Thanks, Mom. I'll figure out a real job eventually. But I appreciate your support. I am having a great time right now, if that makes you feel better about my situation."

Gail paused from washing and dried her hands on her apron. "Like I said, as long as you're happy. It worries me, you know—all the stories of you climbing. Maybe I am better off not knowing, but I am proud of you regardless. Happiness is an accomplishment in its own right, you know."

She opened her arms widely before wrapping them around Pete.

***

Gordon crept up to the small house behind the climber's van, positioning himself to the side of a bay window. He moved slowly over to its edge, just far enough to see inside. He spotted Jeb first, sitting at a dining table, recognizing him immediately from the day his van broke down outside of Thermopolis. Next to Jeb sat the other climber he met that day, whose name escaped him, and seated next to the pair was an older couple, about Gordon's age. There were two more people in the room as well, although he could only see the back of their heads. Gordon sighed—he had been prepared to deal with the climbers by any means necessary to get his packages back but hadn't factored innocent bystanders into his plan. He stepped away from the window—maybe searching the van was all he needed to do.

The side door was locked, as were the front. Gordon pulled out a knife from his pocket and bent the top of the passenger window away from the door frame, using the body of the knife as a wedge to maintain the gap. He searched the brush around the house, retrieving a long thin branch. He snapped the remaining twigs from it and inserted it into the window gap, poking around inside until he found the door latch. The stick bent to its breaking point as Gordon pulled on the latch. The door cracked open.

Gordon slipped in before pulling his flashlight from its belt holster. The interior of the van was a mess—backpacks stacked on top of plastic bins, cupboards so full they didn't properly close, the bed stacked with duffle bags. Gordon started at the front of the van, rifling the glove box and center console, then searching under the captain seats and inside the door pockets. He then started through the bags, backpacks and cabinets, tearing out climbing gear and dirty clothes before stuffing them back in. He was out of places to look inside.

Gordon opened the side door and stepped out. He misjudged the height of the step and fell onto the ground, knocking his breath away on impact. He sat up to recover. A porch light flicked on and Gordon heard a door open. He laid back down and clicked off his flashlight, then turned his head to watch. The old man stepped to the edge of the porch and unzipped his pants to pee. Gordon stayed as still as he could.

When Gordon heard the door close again, he shimmied under the van with his flashlight, hoping the stash was hidden underneath. He scanned the frame and wheel wells and then slid forward under the engine. A drop of antifreeze fell from the leaking radiator and landed on his face. His head jerked upward involuntarily, trying to avoid another drop, and collided with the van's skid plate. He cursed as he crawled out from under the van.

Gordon walked back down the road to his parked truck, debating his options. It seemed prudent to wait out the climbers, hopefully finding an opportunity to confront them without others around. He started the truck and drove back down the road, finding a small flat pullout. "Gawd-damn mess we've made," he muttered as he got out of the Chevy and crawled into the truck bed. He rolled up his denim shirt for a pillow and pulled a saddle blanket over his body, staring at the stars through a crystalline sky. Gordon rolled over and pulled the blanket over his face. It was going to be a cold night.

***

It was the first real bed Pete had lain in for over a year, and it was the single twin bed from his childhood. His feet hung out from over its edge, the down comforter too short to cover them. Lydia was curled up next to him on the tiny bed, her arm draped across his chest. Light from a ceramic Superman lamp on the nightstand washed the room softly.

"Your parents are nice, Petey. Thanks for bringing us all here. You make a bit more sense now, meeting them, seeing where you grew up." Lydia's eyes closed slowly as she snuggled closer.

"Was I really that confusing before? Not exactly a man of mystery." Pete turned his head to grin at Lydia.

"Yeah, maybe not." She moved her head close to Pete's and kissed him on the cheek.

"Thanks for being so nice to them. They really like you."

Lydia smiled, her eyes still closed. "Of course." She scratched Pete's chest softly. He closed his eyes, trying to push the day's residual thoughts from his mind.

"Are you really alright with this craziness? The drugs and money and all. I thought you'd be mad. Or disappointed."

Lydia opened her eyes up, surprised by the sudden question. "Probably not my first choice to be involved, or for you to. But it's done now."

"I know. Like I said, it was all Jeb's idea. The money will be nice though, right?"

"I don't care about the money, Pete," said Lydia. "I don't care if you're broke as a joke."

"What about Joshua Tree? I felt maybe you thought I was too poor, lacked ambition—a dropout."

"Not at all. To be honest, I was a bit jealous that you were going south, climbing more. I had to get back to the coffee shop, my house. And maybe I was a little scared. I've never felt dependent on anyone before, and I was starting to feel like I needed you. It spooked me."

Pete smiled. "Boo!" he whispered. Lydia giggled and nestled her head further up Pete's shoulder.

"Do you trust Dan?" said Lydia, fighting off a yawn. "Do you think you will ever get the money anyway?"

"I think so. You don't?"

"I don't know. He seems a little cagey. But I don't know what he is going through. People in difficult places make decisions that aren't always understandable by those in comfortable ones. Not necessarily bad decisions, not always. But ones that sometimes don't make sense."

"Even if we don't ever see the money, the mission brought us up to Canada, and me back to you."

Lydia lifted her head and narrowed her eyes at Pete. "You said you came up to see me."

Pete startled. "We came up to Vancouver for the money, but I came up to Squamish to see you."

"I'm just kiddin' ya." Lydia reached over Pete and shut off the lamp. "Let's get some sleep Spooky Pete."

Chapter Thirty-Two

Gordon awoke with cold feet, a headache, and a growling stomach. He kicked off the horse blanket and made his way into the cab, hoping he had a bag of peanuts in the glovebox. Finding nothing, he settled for a dip of chewing tobacco and a sip of cold gravelly coffee from the bottom of his mug. It was early still and he was confident that the van hadn't passed by him yet. He started his truck, slammed the heater on, drove down to the I-90 interchange to wait for his prey.

***

As Interstate 90 crests the Continental Divide just west of Butte, Montana, the road crosses through an exposed section of granite pluton known as the Boulder Batholith. This batholith, in places, is rich with copper ore, which made Butte one of America's most notorious boomtowns in the late 1800's. Butte, like many open-pit mines, has since collapsed into a depressing dust of lost riches and pending environmental disasters, but the surrounding beauty of the landscape can't be dismissed. The wind and the rain have sculpted the batholith granite into strange, saucer-shaped boulders, sometimes too smooth and symmetrical to appear natural. These boulders are spread throughout the arid hillsides, sometimes hidden among the sage and conifers but in places so dense that little vegetation can grow. The view of the boulders had captured Jeb's attention.

"What do you know about all these boulders, Pete?" asked Jeb from behind the steering wheel, sipping coffee from his travel mug that Pete's mother had generously filled.

"Not much. I've explored a little bit, tons of problems everywhere you wander. Rock is a bit rough on the fingers for my taste, but the quantity makes up for it."

"Can we stop? Looks too cool to pass by." Jeb looked over his shoulder to Dan and Lydia in the back of the van, who both shrugged almost simultaneously.

"Fine with me," said Pete, "but this is our exit if we are going."

Jeb swerved the van sharply to the off-ramp, narrowly staying on the pavement. Gordon, tailing closely, had no chance to follow.

***

Gordon slammed a fist into the top of the steering wheel as he sped by the exit, the corner of the climber's van only missing his bumper by a few feet as they veered off the interstate in front of him. He had been following too close, and now his carelessness might have cost him the hunt. Gordon contemplated pulling into the median to turn around, but the tractor-trailer to his left was too close for him to change lanes. He pressed down on the accelerator, taking note of the location of the exit to not miss it on his way back. In the rearview mirror, he saw the van heading north on a dirt road. The mountains in front of them would not let them get far, at least not quickly. He sat back in his seat and tried to calm down as he continued forward, eyes scanning for the next good place to turn around. Seeing no upcoming exits, Gordon pulled into the left lane and slowed down until he could enter the median, the Chevy bucking wildly once it left the pavement. He pulled to a stop in the grass while he waited for a break in traffic in the opposing lanes, then sped back onto highway, accelerating as quickly as his truck allowed.

Time seemed to speed back up again once he was no longer headed in the wrong direction. The exit surprised him as he approached it, taking it without slowing down and maintaining his speed even onto the dirt road. The Chevy felt loose on the gravel, like it was floating on air, its back tires occasionally breaking free and drifting sideways. Once the road entered the forest, it became rougher, full of washboard and potholes, forcing Gordon to finally slow down. Ahead the grade steepened slightly and openings in the forest revealed clusters of large, white boulders scattered throughout the rises and depressions of the foothills.

Gordon spotted the van in a small parking area off the east side of the gravel road. He smiled as he pulled in and parked behind it. His patience had paid off. There were a few other vehicles and camp trailers in the clearing, and a man working on a dirt bike propped up on against a truck. Not the ideal place for a confrontation. He grabbed his pistol from under the bench seat and tucked it into his waist band before starting down the sole trail leading into the forest.

***

Jeb and Dan were sitting on the ground under a saucer-shaped boulder while they rested their fingers and forearms for their next attempt. They'd left Pete and Lydia at a cluster of boulders above them on the hill, their public displays of affection no longer bearable.

"The easiest way up the hardest part of the biggest small rock you can find. Didn't John Gill say something like that about the contrived nature of bouldering?" Dan laughed, trying to bite a flap of skin off of his cuticle.

"Think so. Bouldering is absurd, right? Pretty fun, though."

"Pete's folks are cool, eh?" Dan said. "Kind of old school, but they clearly love him and don't seem to judge the fact that he is rolling around the country, living in a van, scraping along with a bunch of other dirtbags."

"Yeah, I see why Pete is the way he is now. I'm still not sure what my mom thinks of all of this. She thinks I'm working my way up the ladder somewhere, first of the Johnson's to make something of themselves. What she don't know won't hurt her, right?"

Dan smiled. "Maybe so. You stay close with her?"

"Not really. I love her, but it sort of feels like a different life ago—that we are different people now with only the family tree in common."

"And your dad…?" Dan trailed off, questioning if he should dig.

"Never really knew him. He beat my mom; she escaped when I was young. He'd show up once in a while and we'd go hide. I was too young to understand, but he was an addict. Pills, I think."

"Sorry, man. Didn't know. Is that why you've been helping

me?"

"Nah— I helped you cause you needed it."

"You are a good man, Jeb. You know I appreciate it."

Jeb waved his hand, dismissing Dan's sentiment.

"Bet your mom would love a call from you once in a while— not that I am one to talk. What brought you out west anyway? Don't think I've ever heard the story."

"Not much of a tale. Started climbing back home in Kentucky out of high school, then just started to wander. Down south at first and then out west. Too poor for college. Washing dishes, backing bar, whatever I could find. It seemed like the further west I got, the more the place and the people felt right to me. Or maybe I started feeling more right, if the difference makes sense to you."

"I think so. It sure feels good for me to be out here in the wide open after too many years in Vancouver." Dan dug in his backpack and produced a cigarette, causing Jeb to raise his eyebrows.

"Can I bum one of those?"

Dan handed him a smoke and a lighter. Jeb lit the cigarette and took a drag, speaking as he exhaled. "I'm really proud of you man. You seemed to kick the habit well. I can only imagine how hard it is—I've said I'll never smoke again about a hundred times or so, and I'll probably say it one more time tonight."

"Thanks. But I'm bluffing, you know. It hasn't been easy—I still feel the urge to use every day. Climbing helps, having you guys around helps a lot too." Dan leaned back onto his elbows. "You know, I never took drugs because I was suffering or in pain. At least no more pain than I think everyone else is in. Maybe restlessness. Maybe dread that this is all there is. I don't know. Climbing filled whatever void it is most of the time, but outside of that, my life had become pretty safe—no consequences to anything. I know it sounds funny, but before drugs I was just as dependent on climbing."

Jeb flicked his ash into the dirt. "I hear ya, man. The modern world is too easy. Maybe we need decisions to have consequences for our lives to feel meaningful." Jeb took another pull off his cigarette. "Do you think we contrive hardship and suffering so that we don't notice the meaningless? Just like we contrive climbing up this measly little boulder to give ourselves an out to the boredom of the rest of the day?"

"Maybe so. If you never have to make decisions with consequences, it's easy to lose sight of the control you actually have over your life. Think about Pete's dad—born and raised in the same valley he lives in now, retired from the first job he ever had. Maybe there is nobility in being satisfied with what you are given—your lot in life—but part of me wonders if he ever knew that he had the power to create a different path. Maybe a better one, maybe not, but one that you control." Dan took a drag and then held the cigarette out in front of his eyes, looking at it intently. "And now here I am replacing one deadly habit with another." He snubbed the cigarette out in the dirt and stood up, dipping his hands in his chalk bag. "Alright, enough philosophizing. Give me a spot on this one again."

***

Gordon found the terrain disorientating. The pines and junipers limited his sight-distance, and the rolling hills and deep channels prevented him from maintaining any visual landmarks as he hiked. On top of limited visibility, each smooth block of rock looked just like the last, leaving him to wonder if he'd been walking in circles. He had crossed over many trails—some were dirt bike tracks, some were more likely game trails—and now he wasn't even confident in the direction back to his truck. Gordon yelled loudly, hoping that he would get lucky and receive a reply. Hearing nothing, he continued walking down the same faint trail he had been on, one direction seeming as good as any other.

***

"Did you hear that? Sounded like someone yelling." Lydia was laying on her side in the forest duff, twirling a twig between her fingers.

"Nope. My ears aren't great though, too much loud music as a teen." Pete was on his back, staring up at the sky.

"Were you one of those *rock and roll saved my soul* types? Cute."

"Hey now, I'm pretty sure you don't want to start in about awkward teenage years, right? I've seen pictures, brace-face. Besides, it was jazz for me. Loud jazz!"

Lydia laughed. "You know anything about musical instruments?"

"Not really. Played a little piano as a kid. Why so?"

"We've got a guy that plays guitar in the coffee shop all the time, he was telling me about overtones."

Pete rolled onto his side and looked at Lydia, confused, but saying nothing.

"It's interesting stuff, at least as he explained it. Instruments produce a shit-ton of different sounds, not just the fundamental note that serves as the base. The overtones are what make the instrument sound unique." Lydia was speaking quickly, her interest in the subject obvious. "A tuning fork doesn't really have overtones, it is pure pitch—but it's boring, right? When a guitar string is plucked, there's lots of overtones. It's these sounds that make it sound like a guitar and not a piano or a harp or anything else." Lydia tried to gauge if Pete was following. "What I found interesting was that some of these overtones don't even sound that good if you hear them by themselves. Terrible even, the guy said. But together, it sounds like music and not just notes."

Pete squinted at Lydia, trying to figure out where she was going.

"So I was thinking that maybe cheesy lovey-dovey shit is like the pure pitch. It's the stuff you think love is when you're young or that's written in Valentine's Day cards. But there is so much more to it, eh? And like a guitar, there are overtones of relationships that are dark and discordant—awful by themselves. But the fundamental note wouldn't be very meaningful without the overtones. You got to have it all together to have anything beautiful."

Pete wasn't sure what to say. His eyes were stuck looking at the ground, unable to respond.

"Shit, I knew it wouldn't make sense." Lydia again twirled the stick through her fingers.

"No, I think I got ya."

Lydia looked at Pete sincerely, "What I really mean—I think—is that I like what we got going on, where we're headed."

Pete nodded, reveling in the moment, her words exactly what he needed to hear. Then he smiled and cocked an eyebrow. "We're headed to Ten Sleep, no?"

Lydia threw the twig she had been twirling at Pete. "Jackass. See if I open up to you again. Should we go find Dan and Jeb? Seems like we better get back on the road if we are going to make Ten Sleep before dark."

***

Gordon heard a car driving in the distance, the first clue to his location in over an hour. He turned and walked toward the sound, making a hill in the distance his guiding landmark. He scrambled to the bottom of a ravine where a creek slowed into a broad marsh, slapping a few mosquitos as he neared. Gordon stepped one foot onto the wet ground, slowly weighting it. When it seemed to hold, he took another step. He sank up to his shin, then fell over trying to pull his foot back out. His boot remained stuck. Gordon rolled over onto his side, pants and shirt soaked with muddy water. He pulled his boot out and crawled to the other side of the marsh.

"Fucking fuck." Gordon emptied the water from his boot. He pulled out the pistol from his waist band, finding the barrel full of mud. He tucked it back in and put his boot on. He started up the hill toward the road, limping as he walked.

When Gordon arrived back at his truck, the van was gone. He had almost expected as much, as any good luck that found its way to him seemed immediately followed with bad. Still, it stung to have been so close. Gordon wondered how long the writing had been on the back of the van—if his luck swung back again, the climbers were indeed on their way back to Ten Sleep. In either case, he had a meeting with an angry Cole that he couldn't afford to miss.

CHAPTER THIRTY-THREE

Gordon squirmed in his chair as Cole stared at him from across the farmhouse kitchen table. His body was restless from his long drive back to Ten Sleep that afternoon, and Cole's gaze only increased his discomfort. Cole rolled the last of his whiskey around the bottom of a glass, the sole bulb in the chandelier above highlighting the rising smoke from the ashtray.

"Damn, Gordon. As much as I hate to admit it—disobeying me and all—you did good on this one." Cole's mouth pursed slightly, as close to a smile as it ever got. "Sounds like they might walk right into our hands."

Gordon relaxed slightly. "Even if they do, we still got a lot of loose ends. Lyle must have told somebody what he was doing for you—Sunny, his uncle...somebody. And now that we got Deputy gawd-damn Dawg and whoever the fuck those other guys are asking questions around town, it's going to get back to us."

Cole smiled menacingly. "I'll handle the deputy and the Fingers. We'll deal with the loose ends as they arise."

"And the climbers?"

"Get our package back. Then teach them a lesson." Cole kicked back the last of the whiskey and slammed the glass down onto the table.

***

Burl crept through the coulee as it meandered around the base of a small mesa. Monty's ranch house was in the distance, unlit even as dusk gradated into dark, leaving Burl to assume that no one was home. The lights of the caretaker's cabin were on, positioned well behind the main residence, but that was a risk Burl was prepared to take. He continued down the coulee as it bent back closer to the house. He had been to the house before, back when it was known as the Circle S Ranch and was actually operational, but in that instance he had been invited.

Burl had taken a few wrong turns trespassing onto the grounds, as he wanted to park as far away as practical to avoid being seen. He was once again operating on a hunch and without a warrant, so precaution was necessary. The gully opened into broad, flat ground immediately below the residence. A few outbuildings and barns were spread out around the area, with a large fire ring and horseshoe pits near the center. At the edge was a tight grove of cottonwoods, with a few stacked bales of hay in front of them. Propped up against the hay bales was a sheet of plywood on which a tattered paper target hung. The ground below was littered with hole-riddled cans and broken glass. The makeshift shooting range looked just like Burl remembered it.

Burl approached the bales, walking in close to the plywood backstop. He dug in his vest pocket for his flashlight and switched it on, cupping his hand over the lens to limit its brightness. There were multiple holes in the plywood, most of them weathered enough to have happened many years ago. All of the holes pierced through the sheet completely. Burl swore under his breath. He scanned the ground behind the plywood before uncovering the flashlight to its full beam and pointing it toward the trees behind. A portion of the bark of one cottonwood was missing, the exposed trunk still fresh and white. Burl walked quickly over to it, inspecting it closely. Near the upper edge of the missing bark he found what he was hoping for. He fetched his multi-tool from its belt holster and unfolded it. He dug a small slug out of the entrance hole, being careful not to touch it directly with his knife. Burl smiled as the bullet fell free into his waiting hand—maybe his theory on ancient practice points was more than an intellectual curiosity.

***

"What can I get you today, honey?" said the woman behind the counter with an expression that revealed that there was nowhere she would like less to be. Somehow, her chewing gum remained in her mouth as it hung open waiting for Chen's response. She wrinkled her nose as she inspected his black felt cowboy hat and creased Western shirt. "Know what you want there, tenderfoot?" she asked again, this time with audible disdain. Urban cowboys were not an uncommon occurrence in Greybull, Wyoming, but Asian ones were.

Chen squinted at the name tag pinned crookedly beneath the orange A&W logo on her shirt. "Uh, hello...Dawn." He looked at her for confirmation on his pronunciation but received only a blank stare in return.

"We will take two cheeseburgers and fries."

"Is that two cheeseburgers and TWO fries? You have to be specific, honey."

Chen nodded and held up two fingers.

"OK. Anything to drink?" she said, with perceivable contempt in her voice.

Chen shook his head.

"All-right, it will be right up. That will be ten bucks, please."

Chen unrolled a twenty-dollar bill from a thick fold of money and handed it to her. The chewing gum hung even more perilously in Dawn's mouth as she eyed the size of the stack of cash.

"Here's your change and receipt," she said, handing both to Chen across the laminate countertop. "Oh, and nice hat. Are you one of them good guy cowboys or bad?" She laughed as he walked away.

***

Pigeon paced around the fire pit, his hands in his jean pockets. The clear skies above the Bighorn mountains had made the air biting cold after the sun had set. He stopped next to Mad Dog, who was lying inside a cotton sleeping bag spread out hastily between the three motorcycles and the fire. Pigeon lit a cigarette before stepping over him, then zipped up his black leather motorcycle jacket and took a seat on the splintered log next to Reno. His expression was mostly obscured by his beard and the darkness, but as the fire flickered he appeared to be smirking.

"You boys complain about the concrete jungle when we are in Denver, but I bring you out here and put you in the woods in front of a beautiful campfire and all you do is complain about the cold." He turned his head toward Reno and winked.

Reno understood the prod and joined in. "But Pigeon, it is

so cold in these mountains, and you built a fire only big enough for you. How are me and Mad Dog here supposed to stay warm?" Reno took a sip of whiskey out of the bottle he was holding and passed it to Pigeon, laughing.

Mad Dog looked up from his sleeping bag. "Are you assholes making fun of me? It's cold up here, and I need to sleep. Too many hours on the road for this muchacho." He laid his head back down and shut his eyes.

"Muchacho? Mad Dog, when did you start speaking Spanish? A white guy from the suburbs calling himself muchacho. Shit." Pigeon took a slug from the bottle.

Mad Dog opened one eye and peered back at Pigeon. "Don't give me that shit, brother. I know you were born and raised in Longmont. Front page news: our heroic gang leader is from a cute little town and has a college degree. Shit, you probably learned Spanish there, in between co-ed tennis classes." He closed his eye and rolled his head back on his pillow.

Pigeon took another swig from the bottle, wiping his lips with the back of his hand when he was through. "Whatever you say, *muchacho*. Get some sleep. We have a big day tomorrow." He smiled as his eyes narrowed. "We've got a snitch to kill."

Chapter Thirty-Four

If the Rose Bowl Parade is horses, marching bands, and roses, the Ten Sleep Harvest Rodeo parade is horses, CD boomboxes, and crepe paper, with a large amount of Coors Light and Copenhagen thrown in. The parade serves as the opening event in a weekend of activity, notably the rodeo itself and the street dance that traditionally follows, provided a suitable band can be arranged and the necessary permits were applied for in time.

The three blocks of *downtown* Ten Sleep were crowded with people—ranchers, roughnecks, retirees, and even a few tourists who took the wrong turn off Highway 20, all watching makeshift floats atop trailers pulled by tractors, pickups, and sagging Cadillacs. The local 4-H group herded a group of well-manicured lambs while the high school dance club performed a routine in the style of a sexually charged NFL halftime show, raising a few eyebrows of the elderly along the way.

The local volunteer fire and county sheriff departments convoyed their freshly washed trucks and cruisers down the street, wives and girlfriends throwing taffy out the open windows. With no wife or girlfriend, Burl had asked his neighbors' daughter Vicky to ride shotgun and handle the Tootsie Roll duties. She happily obliged, as in middle school any opportunity for prominence in front of peers can't be turned down. The pair cruised down the street in front of the fire engine but after a trio of teenagers riding lawn mowers, advertising a local landscaping business. Burl cursed under his breath as the fire engine turned on its siren. He rolled up the power windows of his cruiser to block the sound, leaving Vicky with nothing to do but wave.

Jeb picked up a Tootsie Roll off the street, unwrapping it and placing it in his mouth in a single motion. "I think I like the pony pulling the wagon the best so far," he said, chewing as he spoke. "Super cute."

"Shriners on tiny motorcycles for me, no doubt," replied Pete.

"I don't know, that rodeo clown was sexy. Something about a man in makeup that drives me wild!" Lydia laughed. "How about it, Petey, a little *menage a trois ala harlequin?*"

"That's a fucked-up image," said Dan as Pete laughed, "thanks for that."

Jeb picked up a package of Smarties from the ground. "Man, it's good to be back. I've missed this place. Dan, what do you think so far?"

"I don't know what kind of hillbilly heaven you brought me to, but I'll trust you that the dolomite is worthy. These American rednecks seem to have a little more edge than the Canadian ones."

"Everything is a bit softer in Canada, eh?" mocked Jeb in his best Canadian accent. "Shuuure seems it to me, ya know."

Lydia punched him on the shoulder. "Fuck off, hoser," she said, drawing out her accent.

Suddenly, the fire engine passing in front of them turned on its siren, presumably marking the end of the parade. Pete spoke after unplugging his ears. "Well, quite a parade. You guys want to go get a few pitches in before the rodeo tonight?"

The group nodded their agreement and started walking back to the van.

***

From across the street, Gordon caught a glimpse of Jeb and Pete in between the passing horse-drawn carriage and honking Schwans truck. He couldn't believe it at first, but with a second look Jeb's face was unmistakable. It helped that Jeb was wearing the same faded engineer's cap that he wore the day he hitchhiked with Gordon. He hadn't seen the girl that day, but she appeared to be a part of the group.

His instinct was to hide so that they wouldn't see him, but he quickly realized that he had no reason to—they couldn't know anything. A firetruck obstructed his view once again. When it passed, the group was nowhere to be seen.

***

Cole flinched when the siren turned on, ending his vacant stare, his mind nearly overloaded with stress. He stood behind the first row of people on the sidewalk, but his height gave him a clear view of the passing parade. The horses, music, and straw-bale floats were a surreal contrast to his dark thoughts. He had a headache.

He looked toward the source of the sound and immediately focused on the squad car in front of the fire engine. Burl was driving. Cole stepped forward, bumping into the woman in front of him. She glowered at him but he wasn't paying attention. Burl's car was directly in front of him now. Cole and Burl locked eyes briefly before Burl looked away. Cole continued to stare as his car crept past, but the look on Burl's face was all Cole needed to see.

CHAPTER THIRTY-FIVE

The smell of straw, wood chips, and horse shit hung in the air at the rodeo arena as the grandstands slowly filled with spectators. A tractor was finishing tilling the arena, providing a more forgiving surface for the horse's feet but also the cowboy's bodies which inevitably met with it. A few barrel racers were busy stacking their tack near the outer corral as two bull riders gathered near the bucking chute, spitting tobacco juice and talking about their draw. Their turn would be a while, as bull riding was always last on the schedule to keep people from going home early. People enjoy watching others in danger, and rodeos are happy to oblige.

Dan and Jeb were sitting high up in the grandstand, drinking lemonade and eating elephant's ears, a fried dough confection rarely found outside of fairs and rodeos. In their blue jeans and flannel shirts, the pair blended in with the surrounding crowd considering the social, occupational, and philosophical rifts between them. Their flip-flops, however, betrayed them. Cowboy boots generally mean that the wearer is expecting hard and dirty work, to be riding a horse, or present in social situations where they wish to appear to have ever done any of these things. Flip-flops undoubtedly mean the wearer is expecting leisure, not work, and wants the world to know it. It is a rare individual that owns and regularly wears both.

"Hey man, have you ever been to a branding?" Dan asked as he tore another large chunk from the dough. "Went to one in Calgary once. It's a real trip."

"A what?"

"I guess that's a *no*," said Dan, washing the fried dough down with a sip of lemonade. "It's a big event in ranching towns, in the spring after calves are born. Everyone gets together to gather up the new calves, give them their shots, then castrate and brand them. You eat a lot of food, get drunk, and laugh at teenage boys trying to wrestle down calves." Dan said, placing his lemonade on the bench next to him. "If you ever get a chance, you should go to one."

"Castrate and brand? What kind of barbarians are they?" If Jeb was kidding, it didn't show.

"The only thing barbarian is your hypocrisy," laughed Dan. "You didn't seem to be bothered by such things when you were enjoying your cheeseburger this afternoon—no brandings, no burgers."

Jeb smiled. "That's fair. I did really enjoy that burger. Don't ruin cheeseburgers for me, man. You got me off Yoo-hoo, take that as your victory and leave me with something." He took a deep breath for drama. "Leave me something to live for."

"Don't tell someone still jonesing for smack about needing something to live for."

"Playing the ol' *I-used-to-give-handjobs-for-heroin* card again, eh? Someday you have to move on."

Dan wasn't amused. "Fuck off man. You have no idea what it's like."

"Just kiddin' ya. I'm just glad the heroin didn't kill you so that you can die some equally pointless death—free soloing, a car wreck, or getting kicked in the head by a horse at a rodeo."

Dan finally smiled. "As they say, you can't choose how you die but you can choose how you live. Or something like that."

A screech suddenly filled the stadium as the announcer turned on his microphone too close to the speaker.

"Sorry about that, folks! Just trying to wake y'all up!" the announcer said in a voice from another era. "Welcome to the Ten Sleep Harvest Rodeo! We've got some special events lined up for you tonight, along with all the classic events you expect. We got a national bareback champ in the house tonight, and a great pen of bucking bulls as well. But first, please rise, take off yer hats, and join me in singing our great nation's National Anthem."

***

As the Star-Spangled Banner began to play from the P.A., Chen elbowed Hulin in the ribs and nodded to the cowboy hat still on his head. Chen had already removed his and was holding it over his chest. The pair stood at the entrance to the arena, just off to the side of the foot traffic still shuffling in. Chen scanned the crowd. His eyes moved systematically across each row, moving up to the next row at the end. The anthem finished and the crowd began to sit back down, interrupting Chen's focus. He squinted and started the row again once most people were seated. As his search neared the top of the bleachers, he saw Dan, still standing.

"Double-dealing motherfucker." Chen growled, putting his hat back on. He motioned to Hulin. "Let's go."

***

Pigeon leaned on the wooden bleacher post, using it to hide himself from Cole, who sat in his truck a few rows from the front of the parking lot. He looked across the rodeo ground's main entrance gate to Reno, who was similarly leaning on the side of a concession stand smoking a cigarette. Pigeon's gaze then shifted to Mad Dog back at the motorcycles, parked in the corner of the lot by the portable outhouses. He nodded to Mad Dog to acknowledge that the plan was still on course. If they could stay on Cole until he was alone, the three would easily overwhelm him. Pigeon wasn't sure what would happen after—maybe they would let Cole off easy, try to salvage their business partnership. But probably not. He hated it when people pointed guns at him.

Pigeon felt a cold drop hit his forehead. He wiped it from his skin, finding blue liquid on the tips of his fingers. He looked up as another drop landed in his eye.

"Fuck!" he yelled, rubbing his stinging eye with a knuckle. When he could focus his vision again, he saw a child's face poking through the benches of the bleachers above, smiling. The child's lips and tongue were dyed blue from the snow cone he held out above Pigeon's head. He tipped the paper cone a bit further over, hitting Pigeon with another splash of slushy liquid. The kid erupted with laughter as Pigeon retreated deeper into the grandstands, his previous patience evaporating.

***

The Worland County Sheriff Office's tradition of having a booth at rodeos seemed like a waste of time and government resources to Burl—he had too many loose ends to follow up on to be serving lemonade and glad-handing locals. He was grateful, however, for

157

the cool weather, as the temperature during the Fourth of July rodeo was typically approaching triple digits.

"You solving crimes again, Deputy?" said Earl Baker as he walked by the booth. "What is it this time, some kid steal a cup of lemonade?"

Burl smiled and nodded at Earl but didn't bother getting up from his chair. "Not sure I would prod the law if I was on my fourth DUI," he muttered under his breath. "Asshole." He leaned back in his chair and put his feet up on the booth's table. Burl pushed his hat down over his face and shut his eyes.

***

Cole's heavily tattooed arm was hanging out the window of his truck, his fingers slowly drumming on the side of the door. The fingers of his other hand held a cigarette near his lap. His eyes were fixed on Burl, who appeared to be sleeping in the sheriff booth. Cole didn't know how much Burl had uncovered about his operation, but it didn't matter—he was a threat. Cole's training had taught him to maintain a plan until it was no longer appropriate, and only act on instinct after successive plans had failed or became invalid. Today, he had no plan *A*, no backup plan, and worse, his instinct was polluted with anger. He wasn't sure what he was going to do, but he felt that he was going to do it soon.

***

"What are you doing?" asked Pete as Lydia blocked the Porta-potty door from closing behind him. She cracked the door back open and squeezed in beside him.

"What's it look like I am doing?" Lydia pushed him playfully against the side, then pressed her body against his.

He resisted. "In here? No way."

"Don't be a prude, Petey," she whispered as her lips brushed his earlobe. "It's now or never, those cowboys and their horses have me heated up."

"What? That doesn't even make sense." He pushed her back against the urinal. "And kind of insulting for that matter. Or are you trying to make me jealous?"

Lydia launched back at Pete, this time placing her hand on his crotch as she again pressed her mouth again to his ear. "C'mon. I promise it will be fun."

"It's not even sanitary! Look around, it's gross in here!" Pete tried again to push her away, but she wrapped her arm around his back and pulled him tighter. He lost balance and stepped forward to counter, his foot landing on Lydia's. He caught himself with a hand on the outhouse door. The plastic lock strained. Lydia leaned backwards against the door, her foot trapped under Pete's. The locking lever flexed until it broke free of the frame. Lydia fell through the doorway, pulling Pete down on top of her. Dirt billowed up around them as they landed.

Lydia looked to the side to see two people waiting in line at the adjacent outhouse. She joined in their laughter. Pete looked up, his face blushing, to see a dirty pair of cowboy boots in front of his face.

Gordon looked down at the pair with a sly grin. "Well, it's my lucky day. I must be living pretty good to have the pair of you fall down in front of my feet. And to think, I was just trying to take a piss."

He squatted and lowered his voice. "I've got some questions for y'all, and I think the pistol tucked in my vest will make you interested in answering them. Why don't you two lovebirds get up and follow me." Gordon clicked his tongue a few times and nodded in a vague direction towards the parking area. "Quietly."

***

Burl woke from his nap needing to pee. He stood up with a groan and paused to allow the pain in his hips to settle. A commotion by the outhouses caught his attention. Burl left the booth and walked closer. He saw Gordon squatting over a couple that appeared to have fallen on top of each other. Something about the situation felt wrong to Burl. He reluctantly walked forward.

Cole launched sideways into Burl, tackling him to the ground, knocking the air from his lungs. Cole climbed on top of him and put a knee on his chest. He wound up and threw a punch at his face, but Burl blocked it with his forearm. Burl tried to squirm free but Cole was too strong.

Pigeon ran over from underneath the grandstands, seeing his opportunity. He pulled Cole off of Burl by his shirt, then kicked him in the ribs. A local cowboy saw the commotion and tried to get between Pigeon and Cole but was immediately knocked down by Mad Dog.

Burl was back on his feet, a bit dazed. He pulled his pistol from his holster and pointed it in the air, firing off a shot. The group froze at the sound. Cole locked eyes with Burl, then turned and ran, using the grandstand uprights as cover.

Pigeon, Mad Dog, and Reno ran after Cole, weaving through the wooden bleacher uprights. Burl ran after the group, struggling to keep up. Cole reached the far side of the bleachers and entered the parking lot, his truck parked only a few rows away. The Fingers skirted the remainder of the bleachers and mounted their bikes just moments after Cole sped away.

Burl stopped, breathing heavily. He placed his hands on his sides to help with the splitting pain, squinting toward the trail of dust rising off in the distance.

***

The gunshot was muffled by the time it rattled through the grandstands. The PA screeched again as the announcer keyed his microphone.

"Sounds like someone is getting a little too excited about this rodeo! Ladies and gentleman, keep in mind that ordinances prohibit firearms in the rodeo arena, but if you got one, please make sure that safety is on. Next up in the chute is a real tough bull dogger. It says Chase Withers on your program but most people just call him Thumper. OK, here we go, let's cheer him on!"

The gate opened and Thumper quickly leapt from his horse at the darting steer but missed and rolled into the dirt. The crowd issued their disapproval with a collective sigh as the cowboy dusted off his jeans.

Dan turned to Jeb confused. "Someone fires a gun and that's all that happens? What the fuck is up with America?"

"That's new to me, too. They are real nice folks, they just love their guns."

"It's not the guns that concern me, it's the bullets coming out of them. You want anything at the concession stand, I'm going to go get a lemonade and see what happened to Pete and Lydia. Probably making out under the bleachers." Dan stood up and tucked his pockets further down in his jeans.

"Yeah, grab me a Coors while you're down there, I'll hit you back."

Dan nodded and started to walk down the stairs. The announcer was back on the microphone.

"Make sure you sign up yer kids for the mutton bustin' competition held just before the bull ridin'. Two divisions, ages four through eight. Kid that rides their sheep the longest wins fifty bucks. Ride that wool!"

Dan reached the bottom of the stairs and cut through the corner of the bleachers on a well-worn shortcut, ducking his head under the wooden bleacher frame. Chen stepped in Dan's path and grabbed his throat with both hands. Dan pulled Chen's hands free, sweeping his legs out from under him with a swift kick. Dan saw a flash of gold from the corner of his vision as Hulin's brass-knuckles impacted his skull.

Chapter Thirty-Six

As Gordon led Pete and Lydia closer to his truck and further from the crowds of the rodeo grounds, he pulled the pistol out of his vest.

"Head on over to that blue Chevy," he said, waving his gun in its direction.

Pete looked at Lydia with confusion and fear, wishing that he didn't feel so helpless. As they approached the truck, Lydia screamed as loud as she could in the direction of the grandstands. Gordon kicked her in the small of the back, knocking her down into the dirt. Gordon hovered over her.

"Shut your mouth, or I'll kick you again."

Pete charged at Gordon from the side, tackling him to the ground. Pete was on top of Gordon, their faces almost touching as Lydia scrambled back to her feet.

"I still got my finger on the trigger," Gordon grunted, his pistol pinned under Pete. "Get off me or I'll pull it."

Pete remained in place, considering his options. Thinking of nothing, he crawled off Gordon and stood next to Lydia.

Gordon got to his feet. "Open the door, cowboy. There's a roll of tape in the glove box. Why don't you be a pal and tape your girlfriend's hands together. If you don't, I'll knock you out and do it myself."

Pete slowly opened the door, glancing behind him as he reached for the glovebox. He turned suddenly, winding up to throw a punch. Gordon kicked him against the cab before he could.

"I'm getting tired of this bullshit. Next time I shoot."

Gordon pushed the nose of his gun into Pete's ribs. "Get that tape, ya hear?"

Pete opened the glovebox and grabbed the roll. He gently taped Lydia's hands together at the wrist. Gordon took the roll from Pete, motioning for Pete to put his own hands behind his back. Gordon taped them together tight. He added another layer to Lydia's before pushing her into the narrow opening of the crew cab. Pete followed and Gordon shut the door behind him. He climbed in, started the engine and drove off.

*****

Dan slowly roused, his head swollen with pain. He was conscious enough to understand that he was lying down, gagged and blindfolded. He wasn't aware that he was in motion until Chen's motorhome rounded a slight corner and he rolled across the aisle, crashing into the cabinet on the other side. The pain closed in on him, overtaking him again with darkness.

*****

Where is everybody? wondered Jeb, still in the grandstands. *And where is my damn Coors?*

It had been some time since Dan had left, and Jeb suddenly felt quite alone in an arena full of people. It was time to go look around. He stood up just as a woman was scooting past the seated spectators in the row behind him. As his shoulder contacted with her arm, beer splashed out of the cup she was holding and onto her frilled cowboy-cut shirt. She wiped the beer off her chest and flicked it off her hand with a quick shake.

"If you want to see a wet t-shirt contest you're gonna have to go to Casper, sweetie," she laughed enthusiastically.

Jeb blushed as he made eye contact with the woman. "Sorry, ma'am. Didn't mean to bump you."

"Don't apologize, honey. Most action I've had for months." Her eyes scanned Jeb, bottom to top, and then she smiled with a raised eyebrow. "Say, no boots and no hat? You ain't from around here, are ya?"

"No, ma'am. Just visiting." Jeb blushed visibly. "I didn't think cowboy wear was compulsory at these events," he said. Then he winked. He wasn't even sure why—the woman was a bit older than himself and while not unattractive, definitely not his type. The makeup and sculpted hair, the filled-out Wranglers. He immediately regretted it, quickly breaking eye contact with her.

The woman stepped forward over the bleacher separating the two, her body touching his. She grabbed the back of Jeb's head and pulled his ear close to her mouth. She touched her lips to his earlobe, whispering, "You can wear my ass as a hat if you want to."

Jeb pulled his head away. Her perfume was heavy in his nose, and Jeb was conflicted in the emotions he felt. His eyes blinked unconsciously. "I don't even know what that means," he stammered, as much to himself as to her.

"And as far as boots," she continued as she again pressed her mouth close, "you don't need any because I'll leave mine on. I'll lay my spurs into you like an unbroken colt." Her hand was tousling his hair, a seductive smirk on her face. "That is, assuming you aren't a gelding?"

"What's a gelding?" stuttered Jeb. "Nevermind. Let's back up. What's your name?" Her smirk didn't change, and she said nothing. If anything, her gaze intensified. "Ah, fuck it," he said, "let's get out of here."

He waved his hand forward in front of him, signaling her to proceed. She grabbed his hand on her way past and led him down the stairs and out of the arena.

Chapter Thirty-Seven

Gordon couldn't bring himself to hit the girl even though he suspected that she would break first. It was hard enough to beat a defenseless man, but Gordon thought it better than what Cole might do to the pair or himself if he didn't get the heroin back. Their story regarding the drugs, the Chinese mafia, and the hidden money on top of a cliff didn't make sense to him, but if it was fabricated, it was a pretty good yarn. The punches hadn't changed their story yet, so perhaps it was time to move on to the girl.

Lydia looked up at Gordon from the dusty concrete floor of the sugar mill, her duct-taped hands under her knees.

"Bring us to find Dan, he will tell you the same story. He can take you to where the money is hidden and you can have it. Just stop hitting Pete." Her voice was not panicked nor pleading. It might have even been a bit threatening.

"You're next, carrot top. Would you rather me hit you than him?" Gordon stepped toward Lydia, posing to kick her as she sat.

"Stop!" yelled Pete, straining through the pain of his battered jaw. He had a cut under one eye, a line of blood inching down his cheek. "Dan can lead you to the money. We don't know where it is."

Gordon shifted his weight, as if he might kick, but then stopped. He didn't know what to do. He wished he hadn't gone down this path, but it was too late now. He walked over to the sole window in the dark office and pulled the blinds open. He squinted out the window at the dry grass and sagebrush-covered hillside surrounding the mill. He spoke without turning from the window.

"You think that your friend Dan would give up the money to get you two hippies back in his life? Gotta love the delusions of youth. Old-timers like myself let go of pesky things like loyalty." Gordon paused, thinking of his relationship with Cole and how he got to where he was now. "Only holds you back."

Gordon continued to stare out the window. He was speaking softly, almost to himself. "What makes you think that I will treat Dan any better than yourself? What makes you think that any of you are going to live?"

"Only Dan knows how to find it," said Lydia. "You have to climb to get there. If you kill Dan, the money is gone for good."

"And if I kill you?"

"We're the only ones that know where to find Dan."

He turned to face his two captives and exhaled. "Fuck it. You win. Let's go find this friend of yours."

Some motion out the window caught Gordon's eye—dust plumes were approaching along the gravel county road.

***

With many close calls experienced while climbing and using drugs, Dan thought that he was comfortable with his own death. Now, however, it terrified him. His previous brushes with death seemed like hallucinations—imaginary encounters fabricated to embellish the experience. Now, in this motel room in Ten Sleep, Wyoming, death felt tangible and certain.

Chen was sitting off to Dan's left in a chair identical to the one he was tied to. Hulin was pacing in front of him. Both men had guns and both had been using them to add weight to their blows against the side of his head. Dan was bleeding from his left ear and from cuts on both cheekbones. His head was ringing with such volume that he could hardly hear Chen's question, but he knew what it was.

"Squamish. The money is in Squamish." Dan's voice was barely audible.

Chen shook his head. "Fuck you and your Squamish. Fuck you for bringing us to this shit town just to tell us lies." He stood up from his chair and walked closer to Dan. "This is about more than money, you laowai cocksucker. Fuck you for not respecting our family."

Chen stood up and stepped toward Dan. He said something to Hulin in Cantonese, who responded by throwing his brass knuckles to him. Chen slid them on his fingers and clenched his fist.

Chapter Thirty-Eight

It had taken Burl a few moments to catch his breath and recover from the punches he had received during the fight. Cole and the Fingers had already fled the rodeo grounds by the time he was close to his truck—finding them now would take as much luck as anything else. He started his truck and drove through the parking lot, turning onto the pavement at Main Street. He crept down Main Street in low gear, scanning each side street carefully. At the edge of town, Burl decided to drive by the town's only motel, the Broken Spoke. If out-of-towners weren't camped up canyon or in the RV park, they were at the Spoke. He pulled off Main and drove the block down to the motel. If nothing looked suspicious there, Cole's farm would be the next stop.

Burl slowed to a stop as he approached. He saw a man dragging a limp body into an open door as another man stepped out from inside the room to help, a gun clearly visible in his waistband. They entered the room and shut the door behind them.

Burl steered his truck into the motel's lot and got out, leaving the driver's door open. He ran to the edge of the motel room window, crouching just under its edge. Burl nudged his head to the window and was able to see a sliver of the room as the air conditioner periodically fluttered the blinds. Someone was standing near the other side of the window, another person slumped next to him in a chair. A third paced behind them both. Burl wondered if he should go back to the truck and call for backup.

Burl looked inside again. The standing man punched the

sitting one, his face already bloody. He hit him again. Burl thought back his failure at the warehouse in Denver—this time he wasn't going to give up the element of surprise. He had to act quickly.

Burl crept to the edge of the pane, then walked over to the small flower garden near the motel's office. He picked up one of the cinder blocks that bordered the garden, shaking the dirt from its cavities as he edged back to the window. Taking a deep breath, he spun, retrieving a long-forgotten movement from his high school discus days, and heaved the cinder block through. He squared his body to the hole in the window and drew his pistol.

The cinder block hit Chen squarely in the back of his head, his legs crumpling underneath him. Hulin spun quickly to the window, firing his gun impulsively before he even saw the hole, the block, or Burl. His first shot broke the remaining glass on the edge of the pane, his second shot closer to the center. He didn't have time for a third before Burl's bullet ripped through his chest.

***

Lydia was sitting on the floor of the mill, her bound hands hidden under her knees. The old concrete floor had spalled, the resulting cement chips scattered throughout room. As Gordon stared out the window, Lydia inched toward a large chip nearby, a sharp, thin oval piece a few inches across. She grabbed it with her fingers, then propped it vertically between her heels. She scraped the tape across its sharp edge, cutting a deeper notch with each pass.

Lydia remained motionless after her hands were free, waiting for her moment. She looked around the room, eyeing a long metal bar propped up on the adjacent wall. She didn't know that it was a *spud bar*, used to dig up beets, but she knew it would make a suitable weapon.

She tried to make eye contact with Pete, who was tied to a chair on the opposite side of the room. Between lovers or parents or climbing partners, there exists a facial expression that can silently convey a message of security, that everything will be just fine. Lydia tried to pass that message to Pete, but as both of his eyes were nearly swollen shut she wasn't sure if he understood her signal.

Lydia jumped to her feet in a flash and grabbed the bar from the wall. Gordon turned and stepped toward her, but Lydia had already begun her swing. The bar impacted the side of Gordons head with brutal force, knocking him from his feet. He was unconscious before his body crumpled onto the concrete floor.

Lydia stepped over Gordon's body to Pete, whose eyes were now as wide as the swelling would allow.

"Holy shit. You might have killed him," he mumbled as Lydia untaped his hands from behind the chair.

"I doubt it, but if I did he had it coming. Let's go."

Lydia helped Pete to his feet, his head still reeling from Gordon's blows. She knelt by Gordon and dug through his jean and vest pockets until she found his keys. The pair exited the dark factory into the bright sunlight, only to see the dust plume of an approaching vehicle in the distance. Lydia pushed Pete's shoulders down as she crouched, trying to hide behind the outline of Gordon's truck. The pair crawled toward the truck and opened the passenger side door before crawling in.

Lydia was prone on the truck's bench seat as Pete struggled to shut the door behind him. He pulled it partially closed and squirmed onto the seat next to Lydia.

"Want to get frisky?" she asked Pete, who looked at her confused. "Just kidding. Stay still; if that's not the police it's probably a friend of old grouchy in there. I say we start this piece-of-shit up and hightail it to town. Unless you have any ideas."

"I don't need to meet any of his friends. If it's the police, what do we even tell them?" Pete's voice cracked as he spoke. "That we're heroin dealers? That you killed that guy?"

"It's OK." Lydia put a hand on Pete's bloody face. "We'll be alright."

Their conversation was cut short by the sound of a vehicle pulling in next to them. They heard a car door open, then close. Lydia counted to ten and raised her head above the dash. The door to the mill was open.

"Let's go," Lydia said, jumping behind the wheel and kneeing Pete in the chest in the process. The truck was started and in gear before Pete could sit up properly. Lydia peeled out in the loose gravel and accelerated quickly down the road leading away from the mill. Pete looked behind them through the window. In front of them, more dust plumes were approaching.

"What the fuck?" said Lydia, seeing the first motorcycle approach, then two more behind. The bikes were traveling fast considering the loose conditions of the county road. Pete turned and watched as the second and third bikes passed.

"I don't know, but there might be more people that know about those drugs than us."

Chapter Thirty-Nine

Cole leaped over Gordon's body without much thought—he had more important things to deal with. If he was still alive after he dispatched the Fingers, he would come back and help. He ran down the broad corridor to the back room where he and Gordon's latest batch was currently cooking. He unlocked the door and shut it behind him. A few large stainless-steel kettles were in the center of the room, its walls lined with blue plastic barrels. Against the back wall was a shelf stacked with tools and cooking implements next to a wooden office desk.

Cole had been outnumbered in gunfights before, but he didn't like his chances against the three Fingers. He had a plan to tip the odds. He went to the shelf and pulled out two large jugs of ether, emptying both into the kettle simultaneously. He then retrieved a bundle of bailing twine from the shelf, unspooling it into the mouth of the kettle as well. Once it was submerged, Cole grabbed the loose end of the twine and pulled it over to the back edge of the desk. He then removed a glass container of hydrochloric acid from the shelf and dumped it into the kettle. He was working fast, knowing that he didn't have much time.

Cole moved back to the desk and pushed it out from the wall, trying to create some shelter behind it. He pulled a handcart out of the corner and used it to move a blue barrel to the corner of the desk. After two more barrels had been arranged, he climbed over them into the cavity formed between the desk and barrels. It wasn't the most comfortable place to sit, nor as shielded as he would like, but the Fingers would be on him soon. Cole wondered how powerful the explosion would be, only knowing that Gordon had told him the mixture was extremely dangerous. He wondered if his makeshift blast-shield would be enough to protect him, or if the blast would kill them all. Cole thought the odds were roughly equal, and he wasn't sure he cared which way it fell.

***

Pigeon entered the sugar mill first, gun drawn, with Reno and Mad Dog flanking him. He prided himself on doing just as much dirty work as his generals, but now he went first only because he wanted to be the one to pull the trigger. He tried to run his business without getting tangled in drama or emotion, but Cole had crossed a line and Pigeon was eager to take revenge. The trio walked briskly down the mill's corridor, taking turns kicking in the doors to the adjacent rooms. They slowed as they approached the last room, knowing that Cole was inside.

"We've got the motherfucker cornered like a rat in a cage," Pigeon whispered, smiling.

Cole flicked his lighter alive when he heard footsteps outside. He held the flame with a steady hand above the soaked twine, waiting. The gaseous compound hung low over the kettle, its penetrating scent not yet invading the edges of the room. Outside, Pigeon put his hand on Reno's shoulder, pulling him behind. He twisted his head to nod to Reno and Mad Dog, then stepped forward and kicked the heel of his boot toward the catch of the door.

As the door flew open, Cole's hand dropped to the floor. The soaked twine ignited instantly, the flame propagating down its length impossibly fast. Cole looked toward the open doorway through a narrow gap between the barrels, catching Pigeon's stare directly. His gaze was intense, but calm. Pigeon broke eye contact quickly, his eyes moving to the kettle. Cole could see them fill with panic. The flame on the twine breached the kettle's lip, and in an instant the walls of the room were gone.

***

The scene inside the motel room was as grisly as any Burl had seen. One man dead, two barely alive, and he wasn't sure if there was much he could do to save either. He sat down on the edge of the bed, his legs feeling too shaky to stand, hoping that he had done the right thing. He breathed deeply, trying to calm himself. When his legs felt ready, he stepped outside to radio dispatch.

"Officer Hutchinson here." Burl's voice wavered. "I need an ambulance sent to the Broken Spoke in Ten Sleep as quickly as you can." His radio crackled as he let go of the key.

"Hi Burl," Marlene replied. "I just sent both Worland medic crews to the sugar mill. Jessie Hugh was out in his field and saw it blow up. I was about to send you a page and see if you could go up there as well, but it sounds like you got your hands full. Should I try to divert an ambulance to you?"

Burl interrupted. "No, Marlene. Time might be short here, I'll take these guys into Worland myself. Call the ER there and tell them I'm coming."

Burl put his radio back in his belt holster. He pulled the comforter off the bed and into the back of his pickup. He loaded Dan and Chen on top, shut the tailgate, and started driving west toward Worland, pushing the truck as fast as it would go. Another vehicle approached, over the center lane line, moving just as fast. Burl pulled onto the shoulder to make room, soon recognizing the oncoming truck as Gordon's. As it passed, Burl saw it was not Gordon behind the wheel but a young, red-haired woman he didn't know.

CHAPTER FORTY

Pete's vision was slowly returning to normal as he and Lydia approached Ten Sleep. He had found a handkerchief in the cab and used it and some spit to clean most of the blood from his face, but he couldn't hide the black bruises and swollen eyes.

"What do we do now?" asked Pete, his parched voice raspy.

Lydia shook her head. "I don't know. I think we start with finding Jeb and Dan, right?"

Pete nodded. "Then a glass of water."

They approached the edge of town and the rodeo grounds, but the parking lot was nearly empty, with only a few horse trailers and food trucks remaining. They continued through town, spotting the van parked in front of the saloon. They parked Gordon's truck behind and headed inside.

Jeb spilled his beer on the counter in his haste to get up off as the pair entered. "Where the fuck did you guys go? Oh shit, Pete, what happened to you?"

"Long story. Glad to see you." Pete pulled Jeb in for a hug, his eyes still slits.

"We got kidnapped by that mustached creeper that you hitchhiked with," interrupted Lydia. "He wanted his heroin back. Beat Petey pretty good trying to get us to tell him where it was."

"What? That guy? How did you get free?"

"You should have seen Lydia!" said Pete, struggling to keep his voice hushed. "She hit him over the head with a giant metal bar. Knocked him cold." Lydia mimed a baseball swing in slow motion.

"So he's still out there? Probably really pissed now, right?"

"He's not getting up anytime soon," Lydia said, "but we better come up with a plan. There were some bikers out there, sped by us as we drove off. I think they might be after us too." Lydia paused and looked around the saloon. "Where's Dan?"

All three looked stunned.

"I assumed he was with you," said Jeb. "We were sitting up in the grandstands for a while after you two left. He went down to try to find you. I tried to call him, but I realized his phone was in the van when Colleen dropped me back off."

"Colleen?" asked Pete.

"Never mind. Just a nice lady I met at the rodeo." Jeb's eyes darted to the floor.

"We'll circle back to Colleen later," Lydia said. "This isn't good. We have to hide from Mustache, and we have to find Dan, who doesn't have his phone." Lydia looked at Jeb and Pete for a response that didn't come. "Let's drive up canyon and think this through."

***

Dan had regained consciousness during his ride to the Worland hospital but couldn't gather enough brain function to make sense of his circumstances. Now, in a hospital bed with a sheriff's deputy by his side, it was beginning to come together. He had the sensation that he had been talking—he wondered for how long. He felt surprisingly good, and wondered if the IV in his arm might have something to do with his loose tongue and lack of pain.

"Back to the Triad honor system," said Burl, prodding Dan for more details. "I think I understand that even though you'd settled your financial debt, they expected to be repaid for damaged honor. Is that right?"

"Yeah, that's why they wanted to kill me. I didn't owe them anything. You said they were dead?"

"Yes." Burl paused, not ready to say more about it. "I don't mean to sound irreverent, but from your story I think the world is better off without those two."

"Thanks for saving me. I think they would have killed me. I was scared."

"I've been there too. No shame in being afraid."

Dan wondered how much more of the story he had told the deputy. "I'm done dealing. Or using. I promise."

"You don't have to promise me, kid. You've broken no laws

that I have any proof of. This is a good chance for you to start fresh. I was given a new start after the war, and another one after I sobered up. Grateful for those second chances." Burl smiled. "I am guessing you were promising yourself, anyway."

The pager on Burl's belt buzzed, followed closely by the cell phone in his pocket. He stood up to retrieve the phone. "Hi, Marlene. I'm still at the hospital. I'm sure Sheriff Dawes wants to talk to me but it can wait."

Burl's expression faded as he listened. He slowly sat back down in the chair behind him. "Oh. OK. Dead?" Burl paused as he listened to Marlene. "Sure, I can do that. Here at the hospital? I'll let you know what I find out. Tell Frank that I'm on top of it." Burl put the phone in his shirt pocket and turned his attention back to Dan.

"I gotta go. Explosion at the sugar mill, sounds ugly." Burl extended his hand to Dan, who struggled to meet it with his.

"You've been through a lot, get some sleep. And I know you aren't asking for any advice, but my wife told me this as she lay dying in this very hospital—*There ain't no prize for who lives the longest, only for those who live the best.* Take care of yourself. I'll come check on you a bit later."

***

"Gordon Phillips," announced Burl as he walked into the hospital room where Gordon was handcuffed to a steel bed, halfway reclined. Gordon did not immediately pick up on Burl's overly dramatic tone through the fog of his concussion. "You've got quite a bit to tell me about."

Burl sat down next to the bed. "Let me get these off of you," he said as he keyed open the handcuff lock. "You don't look like you're in much condition to be running very far at the moment."

Gordon was surprised to see Burl, even though his current situation had no foreseen exit that didn't include a visit from the authorities. Even in death the chaplain would have been sent.

"Deputy." His eyes didn't depart from the end of his bed. Burl pulled a chair closer and sat down.

"Simple questions first: How did you end up in an explosion with a gang of drug-running bikers?"

Gordon had no recollection of the explosion—his memory ended a few moments before due to Lydia's blow with the spud bar—so his lie arrived naturally.

"I was just working at the plant, then the next thing I know,

I wake up in this bed." He made eye contact with Burl for the first time. "I don't know anything about bikers or an explosion."

Burl tapped his lips with his index finger, wondering if he should play his hunch. After a moment, he hadn't thought of a better option. "That's not what Cole told me."

Gordon's head fell back onto his pillow, but he remained silent. "Tell me about the drugs, Gordon. If you help me, we will let you off easier than the rest. We want the guys up high—the kingpins, not you." Burl's bluff continued as he grew more confident, even as the word *kingpins* took a moment to dislodge from his mouth.

Gordon sighed, turning his head toward Burl. "I didn't mean to get involved, Burl. I really didn't. But I needed the money, and it seemed like a safe bet. And you know Cole. He has a certain wheedlin' to him that is hard to reckon. I never thought it would go as far as it did."

Burl nodded. Cole's body was currently at the Washakie county morgue in Worland, but he had no plans to tell Gordon that until he learned everything he wanted to know. "So, back to the drugs."

Gordon described the origin of his involvement in the operation, long after Cole had started growing poppies, after he had established a market in Denver for the unrefined opium, after he'd met Satan's Fingers.

"I didn't think Cole's idea to purify the opium would work, but I didn't think you could grow poppies in Wyoming either." A smile was barely visible on Gordon's face, as if he was proud of the pair's success in the venture. "But sure enough, it ain't that different than beets. Except for the final step. That's pretty different. Dangerous, too—easy to explode." Burl's eyebrow rose slightly, although Gordon didn't seem to notice. "It's easy to discount Cole's brainpower, with his background and such, but the guy has a thinker on him."

When it became clear that Gordon was through with this portion of his story, Burl prompted for more. "And Satan's Fingers? They were your distribution?"

"Yeah. I was completely disconnected from that side of the business. I've never met them, never talked to them. I was the cook in the kitchen, not the waiter. Can't tell you any more about Satan's Fingers, cause I don't know more."

Burl's face took on an even more serious expression. "Which one of you killed Lyle?"

Gordon's face suddenly blushed red with anger. "Neither

of us. And that's the truth." He turned his gaze away from Burl and stared at the wall as he spoke. "Lyle was a good man. We didn't have any reason to kill him. He did his job well, didn't ask too many questions. And we paid him well in return."

Burl looked up quickly from his notebook, unable to hide his surprise.

"Cole didn't tell you that part?" asked Gordon, noticing Burl's reaction.

Burl shook his head. "No," he said, speaking more quietly than before.

"Lyle was delivering the heroin to the Fingers in Denver. The horses were just a cover so Sunny wouldn't find out, he really didn't want her to know. Lyle did sell the horses, that part was true. Helped us clean some of the cash."

Burl rubbed his eyes, trying to comprehend Gordon's tale, and decide whether he believed him.

"What if Lyle had been stealing some money? That would give Cole the motive to kill him, right?"

"Cole told me he didn't kill him, and it seemed like he was telling the truth. But with his temper, you never know. You better have that conversation with him yourself."

Burl pursed his lips and nodded. "You bet," he sighed, then looked away to hide his lie.

"Damn it, Burl. I am sorry. I really am. I had no idea where this would all go. I hope those kids are OK. I didn't want to hurt them."

Burl suddenly returned his stare to Gordon, pulled from his thoughts. "Kids? What are you talking about? The red headed girl?"

Before Gordon could answer, Burl's mobile phone vibrated again in his pocket. He looked at the number shown on the screen, then held up a single finger to mute Gordon.

"Deputy Hutchinson speaking."

"Hi Deputy. Leroy Pickens, Cheyenne Forensics lab. I have some results for you on that bullet you sent." Burl walked to the door of the hospital room and stepped outside. "Positive match on the bullet you pulled from the tree and the one found in the victim. They were fired from the same gun."

Burl's face went white with the news. "Thanks, Leroy. I appreciate it." Burl started walking frantically down the hallway toward the exit. "I'll give you a call later to get the rest of the details. Gotta run." He pushed the door open and was nearly running by the time he hit the stairs.

Inside the hospital room, Gordon was rubbing his wrist, red with irritation from the recently removed handcuffs, pondering his next move.

Chapter Forty-One

As soon as Monty saw the sheriff's truck motoring down the county road leading to his house, he accepted his fate. He wouldn't run nor hide. Instead, he rose out of the chair at his kitchen table and refilled his tea mug with water from the kettle. He slowly made his way back to his chair and sat down.

He didn't know how they had pinned him, but he wasn't necessarily surprised. He should have been more careful in his planning, more disciplined in his execution. The problem with passion, he thought, is how effectively it overcomes reason. He wondered if even now his emotion for Sunny was clouding his decisions.

Lyle's death was supposed to look like an accident, not just to the authorities but most importantly to Sunny. While her love for Lyle might have faded through the years, she had still cared for him—enough to never want to hurt him despite any attraction she might have felt for Monty. It was hard for Monty to understand this contradiction. It seemed tragic to him that she wouldn't pursue her desires, that she would put Lyle's happiness in front of hers. Monty viewed the world differently.

He should have never fired the gun. It had never been a part of his plan, only a contingency. It was an impossible track to cover, and it seemed likely to be the piece that was now leading the sheriff to his house. Sunny was gone, no matter what he did.

He thought of that pistol now, hidden in the utility closet behind the water heater. The sheriff's truck was nearing his driveway.

***

Burl knocked on the door again, this time with the bottom of his fist. Sheriff Dawes was standing to Burl's right, his gun drawn. Burl nodded to Frank, who then turned to face the door squarely. He turned the handle, and pushed the door open rapidly as he stepped into the house behind it.

"Hands up, Monty!"

Monty was seated at a table. In front of him was a mug and a pistol. He didn't move.

"Put your hands in the air!" Sheriff Dawes yelled. He slid abreast of Burl, gun also pointed at Monty, who finally turned his head toward the pair as they crept forward. He motioned at the pistol on the table. Burl flanked out further and flipped off the safety from his gun. Monty didn't move.

"I thought I'd save you the trouble of searching for the gun."

Frank and Burl stopped moving, stunned by the sudden confession.

"I don't think I really wanted to kill him. I just wanted him gone." His voice was cracking. "I loved Sunny. But she wasn't ever going to leave Lyle for me." He looked at Burl directly. "I'm sorry."

Burl stared at Monty. He tried to speak, but words didn't come. Sheriff Dawes stepped around the back of Monty's chair with handcuffs.

Chapter Forty-Two

With Pete and Lydia being too recognizable to Gordon, they decided to have Jeb search town for Dan while they scoured the likely camping spots in the canyon. Lydia cut Jeb's hair shorter than it had been in years, and he donned a Western pearl snap shirt and boots purchased at the self-proclaimed *variety* store in town. The disguise was largely useless, however, as they didn't realize it wasn't a stranger's appearance that stood out in small towns, but rather the appearance of strangers. They met back up in town, neither team finding any trace of Dan.

"Maybe check the crags?" Jeb suggested, hoping to convince the group to climb a few pitches while they were there.

"He wouldn't go climbing without us," said Lydia. "I hate to say it, but maybe we should check the hospital."

"Maybe some other climbers have seen Dan. At least we can trust them." Jeb was still trying to sell going climbing, oblivious to the trauma Pete and Lydia had endured.

"OK. We'll go to the crag first, then the hospital." Lydia looked at Pete for confirmation, who nodded. They piled in the van and started up Ten Sleep canyon. The aspens were starting to display their fall colors, their leaves quaking in the wind, the creek below reduced to a trickle. It felt like a different canyon than the one Pete and Jeb had left weeks ago.

"Do you think Dan is up to something," asked Lydia as they drove. "We should have heard from him by now. A note at the saloon or campground. Something. Maybe he's going for the money. Maybe he's using it for junk."

Jeb shook his head at Lydia. "No way. I had a lot of talks

with Dan over the last month—I think he is in a good spot."

"Then where is he? Why haven't we heard from him?" asked Pete.

"Don't know. But he is OK, I know it. Have faith, he will find us," answered Jeb as he steered into the main climbing wall parking lot.

***

Dan was many miles outside Ten Sleep before he started planning his next move. It had been a long day and he found thinking clearly difficult. After leaving the hospital early in the morning, he immediately started looking for the rest of the crew. He went to the camp sites along the old highway, up canyon along the river, and even to the Cloud Peak campground on top of the plateau. Without his phone he didn't know anyone's number, and when he dialed his own number it went immediately to voicemail. All he had were the clothes he wore, his wallet, Chen's motorhome, and a stack of hundred dollar bills he found in one of the van's cabinets. He had been too anxious about the buried money to stick around any longer, knowing that once he found a payphone or a computer, he could relay a message to Lydia via her coffee shop in Squamish.

Dan knew he couldn't get the vehicle across the border, but it sure was a sweet rig. Perhaps former colleagues in the black-market trades could help out. With one hand on the wheel, he opened the glove box to check the registration.

"Damn it," Dan muttered upon finding a handgun on top of a pile of papers. One more thing he should have anticipated earlier. He would have to find a safe disposal site for the weapon, but until then cautious, law-abiding driving was even more important. He pulled the car over to the shoulder, grabbing the gun and stashing it under the driver's seat. Dan pulled the pile of papers out the glovebox and set them on his lap. He was surprised to see the registration was indeed in Chen's name. He kept flipping through the layers of expired insurance cards, oil change receipts, and a car stereo user manual. Folded up at the bottom of the stack was the vehicle title—perhaps forging the right paperwork would be easier than he expected. He pushed the collection of papers back into the glovebox and closed it.

Dan pulled back on the road and accelerated as quickly as the heavy motorhome could. He was anxious and knew that he had to return to Squamish and retrieve the cash before the disquietude would disappear. He still didn't have a plan, but he had a few threads. Forging a title would take his contacts some time— until then, he could rent a car in Seattle to take across the border, providing his passport card hadn't expired. Dan sat back into the seat and turned up the volume on the satellite radio, tuned into an 80's station currently playing "Livin' On a Prayer". Not his favorite song nor era, but at the moment it was perfect.

In the distance in front of him, a hitchhiker crowded the shoulder line. Dan considered picking him up, perhaps due to generosity imparted by his new lease on life. Under the circumstances, however, it was a complication he didn't need. He pulled into the center of the road to make space. As he passed, Dan noticed the odd clothes the hitchhiker was wearing—a hospital gown identical to the one he had been wearing earlier that morning.

"The fuck?" Dan said to himself as he pressed on the brake pedal and edged the motorhome to the shoulder. The hitchhiker approached and opened the passenger door. He had a bruise running across his face and into his hairline, his left eye black and swollen.

"Shit man, do you need help?" Dan asked, astonished at the hitchhiker's condition.

"Just a ride. Could you drop me off at the bus station in Greybull?" Gordon muttered, avoiding eye contact. He climbed in the door.

"What happened to you?"

"Nothing that you would believe." Gordon eyed Dan, whose face was in even worse condition. "What happened to you?"

Dan smiled. "Nothing you would believe either. I guess we find something else to talk about."

"Fine by me," said Gordon.

"I'm John," said Dan, awkwardly pointing at himself with his thumb.

"Thanks for the lift, John. Name's Bill," said Gordon, stretching his bare feet into the floor mat and letting his head fall into the headrest.

***

Dan pulled the motorhome in front of the Greybull bus station and shut off the engine. It had been a quiet drive, neither man wanting to talk.

"You want some clothes, man? I've got some extra in the back, might be an awkward bus ride in a robe, right?"

"Guess it would. Mighty kind of you."

Dan squeezed between the seats and went back motorhome's storage closet. "Try these on," he said, handing a stack of clothes and shoes to Gordon. "I'll give you some space." Dan opened the van's sliding side door and stepped out onto the sidewalk. He sat down on a wooden bench and waited.

Gordon emerged from the motorhome in a black silk shirt and matching flat-front pants, several inches too short for his lanky legs, with black socks and shiny leather shoes on his feet. Gordon's black eye, disheveled gray hair, and overgrown mustache created so much dissonance with Chen's gangster suit that Dan couldn't help but to laugh.

"Better than a robe?" Dan smirked.

"Maybe. Maybe not."

Dan stood up and walked over to Gordon. He reached in his pocket and pulled out a hundred-dollar bill from Chen's roll.

"Here's for a bus ticket, wherever it is you're going. And maybe a meal, looks like you could use one." Dan handed Gordon the bill.

Gordon looked ashamed taking the money but accepted it anyway, pushing the money into the pockets of the pants. "Thanks, I appreciate it." He held out a hand to Dan, shaking it firmly.

"Say, you got a strong grip on ya. You one of them rock climbers?" Gordon looked at Dan with a raised eyebrow.

"Nah. Too dangerous for me," Dan said, laughing. He turned and walked back to the van, leaving Gordon standing motionless on the sidewalk.

***

Just outside of Spokane, Dan again felt the smoldering sensation from inside his shirt pocket. The tiny plastic packet was still there, as it had been since leaving Vancouver. He had carried it with him with apprehension, hoping he would never be tempted to use it, but not wanting to fully commit to sobriety either. Perhaps the withdrawals would be unbearable, or sobriety dull, flat, and meaningless; it was his back-up plan, a quick fix until he was back on track, a parachute in case he started to fall again.

The heat of the ember felt different now than it had years

ago in Thailand. It didn't feel warm and seductive anymore—it was hot, as if it might burn him down. He reached in his pocket, unrolled the window, and threw it out. He smiled and turned up the radio even louder.

CHAPTER FORTY-THREE

As Burl knocked on Sunny's front door he already knew she was leaving. The dreamcatcher that had hung inside the door window for years was gone, as were the lawn chairs from the front yard. The realization jolted him—he was as surprised by her leaving as he was by the sadness the thought provoked. Sunny opened the door. She was wearing sweatpants and an oversized t-shirt, her face short on sleep. The two locked eyes, the silence hanging as heavy as the night he told her of Lyle's death. Burl took off his hat and held it on his hip.

"Looks like you're headed out of town. I reckon you already know about Monty." Burl's gaze swung away from Sunny as he spoke.

"Marlene called me and said he had been arrested. I swear I didn't know. Bastard." Sunny wiped a tear from her eye. "I never slept with him, Burl. I want you to know that."

Burl nodded but couldn't bring himself to look at Sunny.

"I've been planning on leaving for a while, but now everyone thinks I am to blame for it all. I have to go." She started sobbing and reached toward Burl's shoulders for support.

Burl wrapped his arms around Sunny, allowing her head to rest in the cradle of his neck. He spoke only when Sunny's breathing slowed down. "It's not your fault. I believe you." He placed his hand on the back of her head. "You don't have to leave."

Sunny pulled her head from his shoulder and wiped her nose with the back of her hand. "I do. And I am. Gonna go work for Justin's cousin at his bar in Casper. It ain't the Caribbean, but it ain't here." She laid her head back down on Burl's shoulder.

"Doesn't sound like I'm gonna change your mind. If you need help, you know where to find me." Burl pulled Sunny in tighter. "I'm sorry about all of this."

The two embraced in silence, neither wanting it to end. Sunny pushed away slowly and grabbed Burl's hands. "I'll come visit once things settle down. Maybe I'll win the lottery and we can go see the Keys together." She laughed as she let go of Burl's hands to wipe the tears from her face.

"I'd like that," Burl said, giving Sunny a final hug. He put his hat back on but otherwise didn't move. They locked eyes in silence, two players stuck in a stalemate. Burl rocked slowly from foot to foot, digging for words that were buried too deeply.

"Goodbye, Burl. We'll talk soon." Sunny turned and walked back through her door.

***

Jeb stood outside the Maverick gas station staring at the payphone enclosure bolted to the wall. Present was the expected graffiti and a plastic-bound phone book hanging from a swivel, but missing was the payphone itself. He had never used the phone, but Jeb seemed to remember seeing it recently, if for no other reason than the novelty of a payphone that was still in service. Perhaps Ten Sleep was keeping up with modern times more than it appeared.

He dug in his pocket and took out his mobile phone. He'd been hoping to keep the call anonymous, his distrust of police prompting cautiousness. He flipped through the phonebook and dialed.

"Washakie County Sheriff's Department," Marlene answered in her typical disinterested manner.

"Uh. I think I need to report a missing person." Jeb said, looking over his shoulder.

"How long have they been missing? It has to be longer than 24 hours before we can file a report."

"It's been almost a week, I think. Since the rodeo, however long ago that was."

"The Ten Sleep rodeo? OK. Yep, that was some time ago. Come down to the station and we can work up a report."

"Uh, I can't really do that." Jeb was reconsidering the prudence of the call. "Can I file one over the phone?"

"The best we can do is get one started. I am going to need

name, age, and description, please." Marlene opened a notebook and made an entry, taking notes while Jeb spoke until she could dig up the formal paperwork.

"And your name and a phone number to reach you at?"

"Uh. I don't have a phone number."

"OK, should I just use this number then, if that's alright. Looks like a Kentucky area code?"

Jeb's body tightened. He pulled the phone away from his ear and ended the call.

Marlene finished scribbling in the notebook, unfazed by the sudden end of the phone call. "Hey Burl," she yelled over her shoulder toward his office. "I might have a lead on those kids you've been looking for."

Chapter Forty-Four

Two days after leaving Ten Sleep, Dan stepped off the dirt onto the gritty white granite of the Squamish Chief. He moved quickly up the easy initial pitches, only a chalk bag and small backpack weighing him down.

His thoughts became clearer with his increasing altitude. He had started to find the rhythm that had eluded him when he began, climbing with the confidence and joy that come with a quiet, focused mind. Even as the holds became smaller and the feet less secure, he felt weightless. Falling felt impossible, the movement effortless.

He paused on a ledge to admire the view and appreciate how good his mind and body felt. He pushed onward through the next block of pitches, casual and graceful. He reached the large platform at the base of the route's crux pitch, just below the summit. A party of two were re-stacking their rope at the base of the pitch, the leader shaking out his arms in nervous preparation. Dan startled them as he approached.

"Mind if I climb through?"

The pair looked at Dan, surprised that he was by himself.

The man flaking the rope paused. "Not at all. Just don't die." He sounded annoyed.

"I don't plan on it, but no promises." Dan winked as he stepped over the pile of rope below the pitch. "If I do fall, do you think you could toss my body to the bottom of a harder route? Maybe *Ben Wobbles* or *Inflation Adjusted Dime Bag*? I'd hate for my friends to know that I died on something this easy."

The pair couldn't hide their astonishment. "I'm just

kidding. I'm not going to fall, promise." Dan said, starting up the pitch.

He climbed quickly until he reached the hardest section of the route, pausing there to remember the sequence he had done many times in the past. He chalked his hands, one at a time, visualizing the moves. His breathing grew heavy as chalked his hands another time, adjusting his feet on the narrow edges. His focus dissolved as he pictured a foot slipping, a sweaty hand unlocking from its hold, his crumpled body lying motionless on the ledge below, the bag of money hidden for eternity. Dan wiped the sweat from his forehead with the crook of his elbow as he tried to push the thought from his mind. He dipped his hands in his chalk bag one last time and started moving upward again.

Chapter Forty-Five

Take, fucker! I said *take*!" Pete was high on the dolomite wall, legs shaking. The knot connecting his harness to the rope was only a few feet above the last bolt that he had clipped, but Pete was still vibrating with fear.

Jeb, who was belaying Pete, had a large length of slack in the rope between him and Pete. Enough slack that the rope was laying in the dirt in front of his feet. If Pete fell, he would fall a long way before the rope caught him.

"Not a chance, hermano. If you fail, you will fail upwards. But you won't. I believe it—you should too. Keep climbing!" Jeb looked over at Lydia and smiled. She looked concerned.

"Trust me," he whispered to Lydia, "works every time."

"Fuck off, Jeb. Take up the slack! I'm about to peel off," Pete yelled again, his right leg shaking enough that it was slipping off the small edge he was standing on.

Jeb didn't move except to shake his head *no*. Pete repositioned his foot on the hold and with a sudden jump, shot his right hand upward and grasped a large ledge. His feet swung out away from the rock due to the momentum of his motion, but his hand held tight. He mantled his feet onto the ledge before letting out a loud breath of air. He grabbed the rope below his harness, lifting and clipping it into the anchor hanging near his head. He looked down at Jeb. "Don't ever fucking do that again! I hate you, Jeb."

"Congratulations on the redpoint, buddy. That's a hard route you just climbed. You can thank me later if now is not a good time." Jeb laughed. He turned back toward Lydia as he started lowering Pete back down to the ground. "The guy needs a bit more motivation to try his hardest. He is capable of so much more than he thinks he is. Sometimes I almost think he is scared of success. I just provide him with a little extra incentive."

Lydia patted Jeb on the back. "You are a true friend, Jeb Johnson. Wish I had one like you myself. And, you are never belaying me again."

Pete's feet had just landed on the ground when the trio was startled from below.

"Howdy!" called Burl as he approached on the narrow trail. "How is the rock climbing going today?" As friendly as Burl was trying to appear, Pete had considered running until he remembered he was still tied into the rope. Lydia searched the ground for a suitable rock or stick to use as defense.

"My name is Burl Hutchinson. I'm the sheriff's deputy here. But I am not here in that capacity, just so you know. Y'all aren't in any trouble." Burl shuffled a few steps closer, hoping he had defused their visible anxiety. "I want to talk to you about your friend Dan. And my friend Lyle."

Pete and Lydia shared a concerned look. Jeb took a step closer to the pair.

"Mind if I sit down? I'm mighty tired after hiking that hill. Don't know how you do it. Youth I guess." Burl slowly lowered himself to a flat limestone boulder nearby. He took his hat off and wiped the sweat from his forehead.

"What do you know about Dan?" Jeb asked.

"Well, I was hoping that you could tell me where he might have gone," said Burl, "and why he left the hospital in such a hurry. I went back to check on him, but he wasn't there."

"Hospital? Is he OK?" asked Lydia.

"He was doing pretty good last time I saw him. Them fellers beat him up pretty good, but nothing permanent."

"Who beat him up?" asked Jeb. "Was it the same *sugar-beet-farming piece-of-shit* that beat up these two?" he said, motioning to the Pete and Lydia. Lydia furrowed her eyebrows at Jeb, who covered his mouth in a sheepish apology.

Burl looked at Pete and Lydia, surprised. "You mean Gordon? Gray mustache, 'bout my age?" Pete and Lydia acknowledged the question with nods. "He's also missing at the moment, but we'll find him, don't worry." Burl tried his best to look confident with the statement. "Back to Dan—you don't know where he is? He isn't in trouble or anything, I'm just a bit worried about him. Hospital gave him a big bottle of painkillers, and I'm concerned they might lead him back down into his hole. It would be a real shame, with all that he has fought through."

Pete shared a concerned look with Lydia and Jeb, then spoke. "We haven't seen Dan since the night of the rodeo. I am glad he is OK, but I'm a bit worried too. I would've thought he would've looked for us."

Burl pulled out a handkerchief from his back pocket and wiped more sweat off his forehead. "If you want me to put out a bulletin for him, I can. I figure it might be a little risky, though, considering his past. It's up to you since I'm the one who owes you all a favor."

Burl noticed their confused faces and continued. "Was Lyle still alive when you found him? I know you tried to save his life; we found the handprints from the CPR. I thank you guys, trying to save a stranger's life. He was a friend of mine, you know."

"I think he was already dead when we found him," Pete said. "We heard the wreck from our campsite and ran over to find out what happened. I am sorry we didn't stick around for questions—we were just, ah, a little afraid. You know, police and all." Pete looked down at the ground.

Burl laughed. "Yeah, I know. I had a rebellion stage myself. If you are young and you don't mistrust authority, I think there is a chance you haven't really thought about the world too much. Thanks for trying to save Lyle. It means a lot."

"We heard a rumor in town that he was murdered," said Jeb. "Any idea who killed him?"

Burl nodded. "Afraid so—local guy. A transplant, but a local. Crime of passion it appears." Burl sighed. "I've been chasing the wrong suspect for months. Heroin ring, it looks like. Can you believe that—heroin in this little town?" Burl shook his head to show his own disbelief.

The trio stood frozen, not sure what to say or do. Jeb's eyes met Burl's briefly before he pulled them away. "Unbelievable. I mean, this town has a lot of horses, but I didn't think it would have a lot of *Horse!*" Jeb laughed. No one else seemed to understand his reference or think it was funny. The uncomfortable silence returned.

Burl put his hands on his knees and exhaled loudly. "Well, I'll let you guys get on with the rock climbing. Stop by the office in Worland and let me know if you want me to put out a missing persons on Dan. And please let me know if you find him, just to let me know he is alright." He grunted as he stood to his feet. "Take care of yourselves now, ya hear."

Chapter Forty-Six

The orographic collision of the incoming clouds with the Bighorn mountains wrung out their rain in sheets. The temperature plummeted as the cold front settled in, threatening to turn the rain into snow by morning. The days of rock climbing in Ten Sleep canyon were numbered.

The trio were dressed unusually nice for a meal at the Two Bit—Lydia even wore earrings—as they had decided that even with Dan's unknown fate and whereabouts, they should celebrate their farewell dinner in good style. Jeb and Pete sat at a table covered in a gingham tablecloth as Lydia walked to the jukebox to make some new selections.

"Jeb, I'm not sure how to tell you this, other than to just say it: I'm going up to Canada with Lydia. We will try to find Dan along the way." Pete took a pull from the longneck in front of him. "I really wish I could go south with you. Red Rock sounds great, but I think I have to give chase to this romance thing."

"Yeah, buddy. I knew you were going her way. It's the right thing to do. I'm happy for you." Jeb gave Pete a big smile. "I'll miss having you as a constant climbing partner, but there will be more time for that soon. Honestly, it will be nice having a bit more room in the van. Plus, your taste in music.

"Where you going to park that thing in Vegas?" Pete interrupted.

"Who knows. I've been giving some thought to Naughty Bob's offer of getting me on a rigging crew for some of the casino shows. He says they'll let me live in the parking lot as long as I'm discreet. Sweet talk my way into a couple of hotel badges and I'll have pool and shower access. Lots of cruisin' for party girls on the strip, *whoop whoop*."

"That sounds like you," said Lydia as she pulled a chair back from the table to sit down in. "Jeb Johnson: *Ladies Man*. Speaking of which, you still owe us the story about Colleen from the rodeo."

Jeb laughed. "The statute of limitations has passed for that tale, I am afraid. I will take it with me to my grave." He raised his beer bottle in the air. "I am going to miss you two. Lydia, take good care of Skinny here; he doesn't have the body type for those Canadian winters. Pete, let's climb again soon my brother." He winked as he looked Pete in the eye, then Lydia. "Cheers."

Pete and Lydia raised their bottles to meet Jeb's. "Cheers."

"And to you, Jeb," said Lydia after downing a swallow of beer, "take care of yourself. It's been a fucking adventure. Squamish in the spring?" Lydia raised her bottle back in the air.

"In the spring, for sure." The trio clinked bottles again, this time finishing the last of the beer in their bottles before setting them back down.

Jeb's smile vanished from his face as he looked toward the saloon's front door. Pete and Lydia's heads turned quickly toward the entrance.

"Dan!" Jeb jumped off his chair, knocking over a few of the table's empties on his way. "You fucker! We thought you were dead!" Jeb ran to Dan and grabbed him in a low hug, picking his feet off the ground. A few of the patrons turned to see the commotion before returning their gaze to the TV above the bar.

Dan walked over to Pete and Lydia, who embraced him simultaneously. "You owe us some explanations, my friend," said Lydia, "as well as another round of longnecks. You had us pretty worried."

"I'm sorry. I tried to find you—I guess I should have tried harder." A wide smile appeared on his face, "But I've got something for you that might go a long way towards forgiveness."

All four gathered together for a long, swaying hug. Outside in the rain sat a slim black Winnebago motorhome with dark tinted windows, its custom Washington plates reading *DANIMAL*. Inside one of the hardwood interior cabinets was a lumpy stuff sack, still dusted in rich Canadian dirt.

Chapter Forty-Seven

Burl was standing high on the Bighorn plateau, near the Cloud Peak wilderness, carrying his walking stick and a small backpack. He had incomplete memories of the day that he and Lyle had unearthed the Folsom point, but the closer he got the better his memory filled in. He had walked a mile cross-country from his truck, the uneven terrain and wind-blown snow slowing him down. Another storm was threatening from the north with heavy snow forecasted, so it seemed prudent to move faster.

He gained a ridge and it was instantly familiar. He looked down the crest and spotted the overhanging boulder, his pace quickening as he approached. It was as beautiful as he remembered it—the brown-red basin thousands of feet below, the hardy limber pines rooted in the tundra, the snowcapped peaks framing the panorama behind.

Burl took the pack off his back and placed it on the ground, pausing as he caught his breath. He kneeled next to his pack and retrieved a small folding camp shovel. He scooted close to the overhanging edge of the boulder, right where they had found the Folsom all those years ago. Burl punched the shovel into the soft ground and dug, piling up the excavated dirt to the side. His shovel clunked into something solid, not as hard as rock but firmer than wood. Burl smiled, his mind racing. He dug a bit faster, working to unearth the perimeter of the object. He swept off the top with his hand, revealing a plastic handle inset in a rectangular lid. He pulled it out of the hole. Burl bent closer and blew the rest of the dirt from the top of the hard-shell tackle box, the name *Lyle* written with permanent marker.

Dirty devil, thought Burl, sitting back on his heels. Burl unlatched the box and opened the cover, revealing stacks of hundred-dollar bills. *The money you made working for Cole, maybe even a bit you stole on the side, buried here until you had the balls to tell Sunny.* He grabbed a bundle and flipped through it, trying to estimate how much money might be in the box. He replaced the stack and latched the box closed. The storm was getting closer.

Burl reached into his jacket pocket and removed the Folsom point. He placed it in the hole left by the box. But it wasn't right, the hole was too deep—he didn't intend to hide the point for eternity. Burl hoped instead that it would be found again, in some other time by some other person. Burl couldn't define why this thought was important, but it engrossed him. He threw two shovels of dirt back in the hole, then placed the Folsom on top. He put a few more shovel loads over the point and compacted the soil with the back of the shovel's blade.

Burl stood back up and tamped the dirt further with his boot. No words uttered, no ceremonial rituals. Was it for closure of Lyle's life and friendship? Was it a gift for the future to find, a symbolic act of hope? Was it acknowledgement of the thread of history that connects past generations to the future? Burl wasn't sure, but he was satisfied. He grabbed the tackle box and started the long walk back to his truck. He had to call Sunny before she left town.

Chapter Forty-Eight

To the Lakota people, whose historical land included much of present-day Wyoming before being pushed into reservations to the east, *Wiyohipeyata* is the spirit of the west wind. He oversees the events of the evening and is the essence of all endings, including death.

Wiyohiyanpa is the spirit of east wind, who looks upon the events of the day and presides over beginnings. He sleeps in a bed of feathers, rarely rising. Only when he is disturbed does he leave his home and voyage across the land. The sick call upon him to ease their pain and give them peace. Wiyohiyanpa knows everything that has ever been, but nothing of what will come.

It was the east wind that broke Ten Sleep from its frozen winter shackles, thawing the canyon and the valley before the spring sun could attempt the same. A rogue low-pressure system was building below the Wyoming border, hurling fierce winds at the Rocky Mountain front. As the wind pushed its humid air on the western slopes of the Bighorn, storm clouds formed and rapidly deposited moisture. The wind, free of its moisture and upward trajectory, warmed quickly as it dropped back down the leeward side of the range and onto the Ten Sleep plain.

It was a *föhn* wind, an *ice-eater*, an eastern *Chinook*. It not only signaled the end of a particularly dark and cold winter and the beginning of spring but it brought respite and peace. It knew the events of the past but told nothing of what might come.

***

The last of the remaining snow under the eaves of Cole's old white farmhouse was rapidly melting. A few tulips had sprouted, but not yet bloomed, and some of the wild grasses in the fields were beginning to turn green. The wind was shaking the branches of the neighboring cottonwood, its fresh buds barely visible. Inside the greenhouses, tables were overgrown with plants, baseball-sized green tomatoes hanging from their vines, the occasional tomato starting to turn red.

Dan and Jeb sat at the table in the center of the farmhouse kitchen, finishing off plates of scrambled eggs and the bottom of a French press.

"Thanks for all of the help this morning, couldn't have moved all of those tomato plants myself." Jeb raised an eyebrow at Dan, questioning his statement. "Well, I could have. I just wouldn't have wanted to." Dan laughed. "I'll get you some cash next time I go to town, if that's cool with you."

Jeb nodded. "Of course, just grateful for some home cooking, a real bed, and the company. I'd work for free if I didn't need the gas money."

"I'm going to repay you, one way or another. I still can't believe you gave me your cut of the money to buy this place. It's the nicest thing anyone has ever done for me." Dan's face was sincere.

Jeb shrugged. "Whatevs. It was a fair trade, a dead gangster's sweet-ass van for a little chunk of cash. I wouldn't have known what to do with the money, to be honest. It'd be a burden. I'm living exactly as I want to, just a bit more comfortably than before. And now I have temporary employment in Ten Sleep anytime I want to come climb. It's perfect. It was really just an investment in my future." A smile spread across Jeb's face.

"Provided I don't kill off those tomatoes before I can find a market, you mean," Dan said. "No need to count your chickens quite yet—not until the *New Bloom Organic* hothouse tomatoes starts turning a profit."

Jeb took a sip of his coffee. "I've got faith in you. It'll all work out. I can't wait until Pete and Lydia see the place; you've done so much work. We'll have to get them to come climb here this summer, if they ever get back from Asia that is. Any word from them?"

"Nope, not since they left Vietnam. I got a few emails from them earlier, but they seem to have dropped off the edge of the Earth since then," Dan said, shaking his head. "I don't even know where they were headed."

"Sounds about right. Freaking love birds. I wonder if they're even climbing, probably just sitting around gazing into each other's eyes and rubbing each other's shoulders." Jeb looked at Dan in wonder, as if dreaming about a similar scenario for himself.

"What about you, did you meet any love prospects in Vegas?" Dan asked as he gathered up the empty plates from the table and placed them in the sink.

"Forget it. I was too busy to even notice all the girls down there. Climb during the day, rig at night. None of the girls I met climbed anyway, so it was better that way," Jeb sighed. "How's the dating scene here in Ten Sleep? Pretty hot, I imagine, right?"

Dan laughed. "Yeah, I obviously didn't think my way through the Ten Sleep romance prospects before I bought this place. Maybe the summer will be a bit more interesting than the winter, with all of the climbers back in town. It's all good, either way. I'm pretty happy just focusing on staying sober, getting strong for rock season, and trying to raise the best damn tomatoes I can."

"Hell yeah. Those are as worthy pursuits as any." The smile on Jeb's face was genuine. "Have you found any more volunteer poppy plants?"

"Just a couple. I wish tomatoes were as hearty as those damn things. I still need to tell Deputy Burl about those, I'll bet he'll find it interesting."

A knock at the door interrupted their conversation.

"Fed Ex!" came a shout from the other side. "Package for you."

Dan opened the door and signed the driver's pad, then brought the box back to the table. He reached into his pocket for his knife and sliced through the tape. Opening the top flaps revealed newspaper written in Asian script.

Jeb pushed his chair back from the table, its legs screeching on the floor.

"Don't touch that! It's from the Triads," said Jeb, standing out of his chair.

Dan leaned his head closer to the newspaper. "It's not Chinese. I think it might be Korean." He dug further in the box and extracted two smaller boxes from the newspaper packing, with a note taped to the larger one.

"It's from Pete and Lydia," Dan said, smiling at Jeb. He read the note aloud.

Dan,

Greetings from Asia! Lydia and I have made our way to Korea, via Thailand, Vietnam, and a quick stop in Taiwan. We are currently in Seonunsan, a place that I remembered Jeb saying had good climbing. He was right—it's amazing limestone! But it's making us miss Ten Sleep. Lydia got her hardest redpoint to date here, a route named Koro Disorder—steep, pumpy, incredible! I wish you and Jeb were here with us, it's been so great. Trip of a lifetime. Thanks for everything you did for us that allowed it to happen.

We will be back soon. We are going to spend spring in Squamish and then come visit you. And hopefully track down Jeb then as well.

There is a carbon-steel knife of traditional Korean-make for you. It's the sharpest we have ever used and think it will be great for slicing tomatoes for BLTs. Speaking of which, did you know that Europeans thought tomatoes were poisonous when they first were brought back from South America due to bad taxonomy? Funny shit. I got loads of tomato trivia for you when we visit.

Also in the box is a jar of gojuchang for Jeb, give it to him next time you see him. We owe him greatly for the introduction to Korean cuisine, and the inspiration for this trip. Send him our love.

Love you brother, hope you are well.
Pete & Lydia

Chapter Forty-Nine

The scent in the air was unfamiliar to Burl but pleasant, thick and briny. The sea breeze gusted, knocking the oversized straw hat off his head and onto the sand below. Burl leaned over in his chair and retrieved it, stowing it on his lap and kicking his feet up on the plastic stool in front of him. He wiggled his toes in his new flip-flops, still not sure he understood their appeal, but wearing cowboy boots with shorts just didn't make sense.

Burl took a deep breath and closed his eyes, the sun feeling like a space heater on his bare shoulders. His mind was blank and it felt great—it had been a long time since he had been so tranquil. His meditation was interrupted with a cold hand on the back of his neck.

"Another marg, sweets?" Sunny asked, swinging around his chair and moving Burl's hat before taking a seat on his lap.

"No, thanks. I'm sticking to my quota. I'll take another plate of those conch fritters though if you're heading up to the bar."

"Sure thing. I'd better hustle though; lookin' like another beautiful sunset." Sunny stood up and shuffled through the sand to the open-air bar behind their chairs. Burl shut his eyes again, wondering if he should go fishing in the morning.

All my love to Hannah and Cy. Thanks for the support and inspiration.

Thanks to Jeff Jackson for the editing, ideas and advice, Lizzie Dalton for the amazing cover art, Jennifer and Mark for the proofreading, and all the other early readers for telling me it wasn't done yet.

Note: Historically, names of climbing routes have often been intentionally offensive, sexually explicit, or pertaining to drugs—a remnant of climbing's countercultural and rebellious origins. The route names in this book are fictional (with the exception of The Grand Wall, Cathedral Traverse, and North Ridge) and follow this tradition. Racist, homophobic, or misogynist route names should not be tolerated, but if climbing isn't gritty, raw, absurd, and a little bit dangerous, it has lost part of its soul.

C.W. Smith grew up near the Pryor Mountains on the
Montana/Wyoming border and currently lives in Bozeman.